FLOWERS AND THE FAR REALM

A DEATHLESS LOVE NOVEL

ZORA FOX

WELCOME TO THE EIGHT REALMS

A land of gods and goddesses—a savage, beautiful collection of islands in the Corae Sea. The stories here are violent, with explicit sexual content not intended for anyone under 18. These books about deathless love feature dark, often twisted romances. Enter at your own risk.

ZENIA

Ruled by Thenios, God-King of lightning

APHRISO

Ruled by Cytherea, goddess of pleasure

ERISET

Contested land, ruled by Ares and Bellona, god and goddess of war

MENOS

Ruled by Scira, goddess of wisdom

NALIA

Ruled by Basileus, god of the ocean

HYPERION

Ruled by Lox, god of the sun

KANTHAROS

Ruled by Vesta, goddess of hearth and home

FAR REALM

Ruled by Hades, god of the dead

Content warnings for this story of deathless love: murder, blood, death, language, and explicit sex including MFM scenes

PERSEPHONE

A slow, wicked grin spread over Dracon's face. His flinty eyes took in all of her, and she lost herself in their stormy depths. When his gaze trailed lower, she flushed. He stared as though he wanted to devour. It was improper. It was intoxicating.

She wanted to run but, for some reason, she stepped closer. Had he placed a spell on her? Something certainly tethered her to him. Whether it was his vampire power or the sultry perfection of his looks, she couldn't be sure. But now, as he bit his lip in appreciation of her form, she wondered what it would be like for her to bite him instead. Indecent images flashed through her mind before she could stop them, of Dracon ripping open the front of her dress, of her straining underneath him as he topped her, of—

"Seph!"

I jumped and had to catch my breath. Heat bloomed in my cheeks as I set the book down. I'd learned to keep a cup of water near the chair where I took my breaks for moments just like this. I took a sip before answering.

"Be right there!"

I wanted to see if Dracon and Esmeralda would finally succumb to their passions. Not what I should be reading about, my mother would say, but I loved stories about dark lovers and midnight trysts. Neither of those existed in my real life, so I lived through others, pretending I could be longed for by someone as beautiful and dangerous as Dracon. Half-ashamed of my fantasies, I couldn't help but be addicted to that moment that made me roll my lips inward and hold my breath.

I spent any free time I could muster between helping my mother and working the royal gardens trying to find more books, creating a little world of my own. It took years. But here was the fruit of my labor.

I read romantic stories in this romantic little shack. At least, it was as romantic as I could make it. Small, once a garden tool shed, it now housed a flurry of plants and flowers. The air smelled thick with them. At one end, I'd propped a bright blue cushion and, beside it, a repurposed half-column that served as a table. Above the little seating area, I'd hung a painting of two humans kissing in the rain. Ridiculous really, but this was my oasis. Things I'd found and scrounged and saved for away from Mother's watchful eye. A place where I could be myself.

I straightened my yellow dress, tied the green gardener's apron back on, and swept outside. Trees covered the entrance to my hideaway. I peered through the branches to make sure no one was looking in my direction before emerging. As far as I knew, no one knew about the converted shed and, although I doubted anyone would want to share it with me, it felt more delicious as a secret.

I found the source of the voice that had called for me.

Libera, the head gardener, spotted my approach and paused shearing the hedges. Her bronze skin sheened with sweat in the heat. A wide-brimmed hat shaded her already dark eyes. While I preferred bright colors, Libera seemed to be offended by anything but earth tones. Today, she wore brown. Once, I'd tried to argue that all shades were earth tones, but Libera wasn't amused. She also didn't agree with fostering wildflowers in the queen's manicured garden. I saw one bright bloom lying in the basket of leaf scraps she'd perched atop the square-edged shrubbery.

"I'm here," I said, trying not to frown at the shears. The hedges looked better with a few more flowers in them, I thought. "I didn't think I was taking extra time on my break."

But I'd been wrong before. Stories transported me out of time. I *hoped* I wasn't late.

"Well, you were," Libera replied drily.

"I'm sorry." I dipped my head in remorse. "Where do you need me now?"

Behind Libera rose the magnificent walls of Epaville Castle, seat of the human queen Vesta-kori. The façade had been carved and perfected, from the roof to the base. As gorgeous as it was, I preferred a little more wildness. Maybe even less perfection. The servants themselves, marching down the stone steps to set out the queen's midday tea, looked a little too perfect.

Everyone the human queen employed were demi-gods. Our arrangement was unique in all the Eight Realms, as far as I knew, but it had the blessing of the goddess Vesta. Visitors from other Realms traveled to admire our gardens. Perhaps

Libera was right when she prevented me from running too riotous with my flowers.

"Check the queen's bouquet." She leveled a look that reminded me I'd almost missed that crucial duty. "And then I have you in the Delphinium Close."

I enjoyed delphiniums but I had to keep them in such neat rows that I felt the urge to apologize whenever I tended the Close.

"Of course, Libera." I dipped my head again in apology as I scurried up the steps to the queen's private patio. Giant flagstones, each emblazoned with the goddess's symbol of two nested V's, ended in a strict line that fed onto neatly trimmed grass, an overlook of sorts. The lawn was just large enough to have a picnic or throw a garden party, but it ended in a sharp drop, though short. Enough to hurt if I wasn't paying attention, since the patio rose about my height above the rest of the gardens. Which wasn't saying much, since I stood shorter than everyone except the queen herself.

From the overlook, I had to admit the gardens looked magnificent. Libera conscientiously tended to the intricate maze of hedges, branching like leaf veins or geometrical butterfly wing designs. Red and white flowers erupted bright as flames from their assigned positions. The arborist kept the trees uniform and thriving. No wonder visitors longed to see it.

I turned my attention to the little circular table placed on the edge of the flagstones. From a seated position, the queen could feel like she was actually in the grass as she looked out. The bouquet in the center blossomed with pale pink peonies, but something else intruded on today's bouquet too. Velvety dark spots added dimension. Intrigued, I drew closer, preparing my power. The dark flowers looked even more beautiful close up. We had a small row of black satin petunias, but I'd never seen them included in the queen's bouquet. Had someone made a mistake?

I looked over my shoulder, but nothing else seemed amiss. So I set my fingertips, light and searching, on the petals and began my work. That brown petal was dying, spreading its dry death to the rest of the outside layer. With a soft caress, I injected some of my life into it, reviving the flower to full life. The black satin petunias were surprisingly healthy—not a hint of decay—but my hands returned to them anyway. Their petals felt so hypnotically soft. A tiny part of me liked the queen more for having chosen them.

The job finished in seconds. Now the bouquet looked perfectly fresh and full. Beautiful.

Movement caught my eye as I started to turn away. A moth trundled out from the canopy of flowers. How had I not sensed it? The queen wanted no bugs at her picnic. One of the other servants usually created a subtle pocket of impermeable air around her as she ate. I didn't see him around. No one else could conjure the barrier.

"Come here," I coaxed, drawing the moth onto my finger. Its gray wing had a piece missing. No wonder it walked unevenly. I stroked its wing lightly, using more of my power than I had on the flowers, and the injury repaired itself. My lips curved in a smile as I lifted the moth into the air.

Just in time. The moment I descended the stairs, the queen, escorted by handsome demi-god attendants, emerged from the castle in finery to take her afternoon tea.

THE ECLIPSE HAPPENED ABOUT EVERY TEN YEARS. WITH THE eclipse came visitors from Zenia, the God-King's Realm. It wasn't an inspection, but Libera always treated it as one. I knew why she got uncomfortable, so I tried for the next couple days to be on time and accurate in my work.

Visitors doubled our work in the gardens. We had to welcome certain guests and disappear in front of others. I had no time to escape to the little shed to read what happened to Dracon and Esmeralda. I imagined they were finally kissing somewhere.

And then there was the census. That was the part Libera feared. Half the time the facilitators didn't bother with demi-gods they'd already talked to, focusing instead on the possibility of demi-gods who had been born since the last eclipse. But sometimes officials from Zenia asked each god and demi-god about their abilities to update information in their records.

"It's so they can control us," grumbled Thorea, picking a leafy twig out of her unruly black curls.

Libera hummed in agreement so sharp that I doubted anyone could disagree.

Four of us—Thorea, Libera, a male gardener named Simos, and myself—sat on the outskirts of the garden to munch our midday meal as we stayed out of the way. Hera, the God-King's wife, was visiting today with some friends. All staff needed to become invisible. The human queen had ordered us to eat our meal nearby because the census official was due today too. The combination put everyone on edge.

I glanced into the trees where my little reading shack hid just out of sight.

"If they know about all our abilities, they can use them as they see fit," Thorea continued. She'd drunk more sparkling clementine juice than usual.

"Do people really get reassigned?" I asked.

"It happens," Libera answered darkly.

I spread my fingers over the picnic blanket. Without her, I could grow my wildflowers, but I'd hate for Libera to be reassigned only because *she* would hate it so much. She could stand to be less overbearing sometimes, but Mother said I needed structure. That was exactly what Libera gave me. She meant well. At this point, she was like a second mother to me.

"Of course we can get reassigned," Thorea sneered. "The gods have absolute power."

"But Vesta—"

"She's not as ruthless as some," Libera cut me off. "But if someone like the Twins demanded it..." She let the thought hang threateningly in the air.

It was true. The Twins who fought over in Eriset could steal who they wanted. They were too bloodthirsty to argue against. My blood chilled.

"They won't do that," Simos said, diplomatic. As the oldest of us all, he was the only one who could calm Libera and Thorea when they got jittery. "You think they'd come all the way here just to get you?" He raised his eyebrows and took a bite of sweet bread.

"Yes," Thorea muttered.

Simos shot her a wry look. "We're gardeners. The officials will probably meet with the queen and the goddess, ask a few general questions, and then leave."

Libera chewed her lip.

"I bet he's right," I said, setting a hand on Libera's knee.

She pulled away, more startled than annoyed, as if she'd forgotten I was there.

I set my hand on the grass beside the blanket, sensing a few broken blades. Idly, I fixed them. A tiny yellow flower bloomed between the gaps in my fingers.

"We'll be fine," Simos said.

"As long as Hera doesn't find anything to criticize," Libera said, glaring at the yellow flower.

I'd been good. I hadn't spoiled the angles and neatness of the garden in weeks. Swallowing down my frustration, I plucked the yellow flower and set it behind my ear.

With both Hera and the census official on the way, I had to be even more careful. The idea stifled me. At a certain point, where was the life in a garden if the plants weren't allowed to *be*?

I finished my tea and stacked the porcelain dishes. "I'll meet you back in a few minutes," I said, smoothing out my skirt as I rose. Today I desperately needed Dracon and Esmeralda.

Before I'd even disappeared into the nearby trees, the three of them were talking as if I'd never been there.

As exciting as the visitors were in theory, they weren't as much fun in practice. Only stress and work increased in the days leading up to their arrival, and when they finally did come, nothing interesting happened.

Hera didn't visit the gardens for long. One walk around the grounds with Vesta herself, and then she left. Libera practically seethed at me to stay hidden, so I didn't get to see either goddess. I would have preferred to escape with my book, but Libera wanted to keep her eyes on me. Maybe it was because of the bright pink dress I wore. I wasn't trying to be noticeable. I just liked color. Libera acted as if one flash of pink in the wrong place would get us all executed.

A couple days later, when our turn for the census came, it turned out Simos was right. Partially.

Each of us had to name our special abilities for the facilitator, but there weren't any prodding questions or meaningful looks. When Libera said she could make anything level or straight, I fought to keep my expression even. That didn't sound like a demi-god ability to me. If she was going to lie, wouldn't it be better to invent a more plausible option?

But the censor didn't question it. Libera was safe for another decade.

Peaceably sharpening her blades with a thought.

At night, when I returned to Mother's house, she asked the same questions Libera would have if she didn't watch me all day: Did I do my work well? How are the gardens looking? Who are you working with? You know the visitor who winked at you only likes you for your looks, right? And you can't give him what he wants, so just forget about it.

Mother loved the gardens as much as I did, but she worked in the grain fields outside the palace grounds. She had a knack for growing abundant crops, and the surrounding area depended heavily on her.

Flowers in rows.

The queen's bouquet.

My reading shed.

Mother and Libera making sure that I behaved.

If I was honest, I wanted a place where I could use more of my ability, where flowers ran riotous and no one cared if I wore the brightest dresses. Maybe someday.

2

HADES

Once upon a time...

No. Fuck that. My life was never a fairy tale. A long time ago when there were fewer gods and a savage cluster of islands, my brother declared himself the all-powerful ruler and divvied up the land among us. I was never his favorite, never saw him as the true mastermind behind the Great Victory that left us in charge, so he sent me to the Far Realm. It was barely close enough to be called part of the Eight Realms, but I figured he liked it that way. His God-King status could reach farther. Besides, he never admitted to fearing me, but he saw what I did in the war, so I had my suspicions.

I manned the deathless prison—not an easy task—and set up my own kingdom. The Far Realm, it turned out, was enormous. I never told anyone. In fact, I actively thwarted any attempts to chart it unless my own cartographers did it. *I* had to know what was there. No one else had to learn about the silver and jewel mines, or the winter forests, or anything else about my property. They knew I was wealthy and dangerous. That worked for me.

And the Far Realm was dangerous. After being unceremoniously ousted to the far reaches of my brother's territory, I found... not a soft spot, but more a direction for my spite in accepting all the rejected demi-gods and creatures. The malformed and terrifying.

Even the dead.

The war in Eriset gave me too much opportunity to make good on that offer. For the price of two coins, I'd accept human corpses if they were sent across the sea to me. Some of them still had their spirits attached. I did what I could to give them an afterlife. No one was so thoroughly rejected than the dead. There wasn't enough manpower to help them all, but I did what I could.

With the war heating up, corpses arrived every day. My workers couldn't keep up with demand. Some of the spirits themselves helped me, an ever-growing business of souls, but I could see them wearing down every time a spirit disconnected before we could glean it. Even my considerable resources stretched to the breaking point trying to deal with this problem, and it wasn't going to let up soon.

I hated asking for help. Hated it. And no one offered. I preferred to be left alone to rule my kingdom the way I wanted. But now I needed someone else who could capture the human spirits or even reanimate the bodies that were still intact.

I exhausted myself trying to manage the whole load—the dead, the prison, the unpredictable demi-gods. Taming myself was one of the most difficult tasks. Now, finally, I had to do something about all of it.

Sitting on my throne beside the eight other rulers—yes, eight (Ares and Bellona constantly fought for control of Eriset)—I crossed my ankles. I'd only come to this godsforsaken eclipse gathering because I was out of options. Unfortunately, though, that meant I had to sit through inane meetings and distasteful ascension ceremonies. The chamber grew dark as the planets cast the sun in shadow.

Lox, that golden boy, literally glowed beside the God-King, casting the only light. If he hadn't nominated two beings—a demi-god and a human—for ascension to godhood, this meeting could have adjourned and I could finally ask the only question on my mind: Were any new abilities discovered in the census?

But that would have to wait. Below us, a priestess offered water to the couple Lox had nominated. It came from the sacred spring that had conferred godhood to all of us, probably, at one time. I didn't remember. More than one human spirit asked where I had come from. What a stupid question... Nobody remembered their own birth.

I dimly recognized the demi-god. Eros, Cytherea's son. He had massive white wings. A much smaller human girl stood beside him. After they both drank, they headed to the altar for a death-sacrifice. Evidently, Eros had forgotten he needed to bring one. That was fine with me. I didn't like to see more bloodshed than I had to. People assumed I liked death, being the god of death and all, and I didn't correct anyone.

I drummed my fingers on the armrest of the throne as the two disrobed and got on the rectangular altar by the spring.

Glancing up at the skylight, pale constellations painted like outward-facing fractures in the marble, I quirked my lips to the side. At least this wouldn't take long. Either they'd find their little death by the end of the eclipse or they wouldn't and they'd have to try next time. In ten years. If they survived.

I didn't have particularly high hopes. It was an unforgiving world.

The worst thing about this display was my brother Thenios' obvious enjoyment of it. A glance showed me that he didn't miss how well hung Eros was. Thenios even leaned forward a little as Eros thrust his face between the girl's thighs.

I tried not to pay so much attention. I'd seen a hundred of these ceremonies. I hadn't come here to gawk at a pretty couple. I had serious business to attend to. Most of the others seemed to regard these meetings every decade as an opportunity to party and socialize. Half the time, I didn't come at all. Too bad for the nominees for godhood in those years. Honestly, I could do without any more beings who were truly deathless.

Thrusting against each other now, the panting couple emitted whimpered cries. Eros' white wings contracted around them, sheltering the woman from view. I shot another glance at my brother, whose interest hadn't abated.

Annoyingly, the crotch of my tailored trousers bulged with arousal. I ground my teeth. *Just breathe through it.*

Deep within, I sensed a claw running along the inside of my belly. A question. The answer was no. Glowering, I held myself at bay.

A life of celibacy wasn't what I would have chosen for myself, but it was for the best. Unlike my siblings, I couldn't simply bed someone and move on. Many reasons. My obsessive side came out at inconvenient moments, I had no time, and perhaps most importantly, I respected my subjects enough not to expose them to my unpredictable darkness unless their conduct warranted punishment. My subjects respected me and I wanted to respect them. No one else had. Weighed on a scale, the health of my kingdom mattered more than a good fuck. Even if I sometimes really, *really* wanted a good fuck. It had taken years to leash the creature within, to make him obey. I wouldn't undo all that because I wanted sex. Denying myself didn't improve my mood, but it did make my efficiency knife sharp. My high-risk population needed every ounce of my attention.

Besides, no one wanted to live in the "horrible" Far Realm with monsters and an emotionally unavailable partner with... dark tendencies.

The couple on the altar reached a fever pitch. Reluctantly, I found myself watching them. They were sensual together, playing each other like instruments. It helped that they were both undeniably gorgeous. She writhed. He thrusted. Then, her head snapped back, mouth open. In Lox's glow, sweat gleamed on her neck. With a loud grunt, Eros peaked too, finishing with a frantically pumping hand along the hard length of his cock.

I let out a sigh, subtly adjusting my position on the throne. At least that was over.

Now onto business.

3

PERSEPHONE

"I don't think I fit in very well," I admitted while Mother expertly scored the top of three bread loaves. Morning sun slanted into the kitchen, drawing harsh lines across Mother's strong arms.

She finished making the cuts before turning her attention to me. "What do you mean? You said you've been working hard, doing everything Libera tells you to do. I'm sure Queen Vesta-kori is pleased with your work."

I shook my head. I wore another yellow dress today, this one longer with a belt that looked like blue flowers. When I spun, it swished. I tugged up the neckline, which dipped lower than my other dresses, before answering. "It's not that. I just don't feel like I can talk to anyone."

"You can talk to me." She smiled warmly.

I smiled back, but she didn't really understand what I was saying.

She muscled the wooden paddle with the loaves into the oven opening and dusted off her hands. "The palace is just down the road. Let me walk you today."

"But, your bread," I protested. I didn't want to say that if she escorted me to work, I'd feel even more sheltered and confined, separated from everybody else.

"It will be fine." She gathered up her long brown hair and began braiding it over her shoulder as she headed for the front door. "You're going to be late."

I still had enough time, I thought, but I didn't argue. I hustled after her. It wasn't that I didn't appreciate Mother—I did, deeply—but I also didn't want her to baby me. I was young by deathless standards, but that didn't mean I needed her to clear every rock from my path.

We walked in familiar silence down the well-worn path to the garden wall. Our home technically lay on the palace grounds, though it was outside the garden, which was why I hadn't covered it completely in flowers. It would be charming that way, like something out of a book. I had to content myself with the reading shed, but I hadn't seen that in days.

When I creaked open the gate, Libera practically threw herself at me. I flinched back, chancing a look at Mother.

"What is it? Am I late?"

"Come in! Come in!" she whispered loudly, hauling me forward.

Mother, concerned and curious, followed me too.

"What is it?" I repeated.

"There's a visitor with the queen," Libera hissed. Her normally tan skin looked white.

Ice slithered down my spine. "Who?" If it was one of the war gods to take Libera away...

"Lord Hades."

Mother scoffed. "That can't possibly be. You're mistaken."

Libera drew herself up. "I *saw* him a second ago."

"Someone who looked like him."

The head gardener was angry now. "Go look if you don't believe me!"

"What would Hades be doing here in Kantharos? He never leaves the Far Realm."

"He does during the eclipse."

Mother never let me go to eclipse festivals, so the astrological event wasn't as important in our household as it was in most of the Eight Realms. Too much debauchery, Mother said.

"*Sometimes,*" Mother said. She was frightfully tall and gazed down at Libera with as much authority as she could muster. "That still wouldn't explain why he was here and not in Zenia." She gave a little laugh, as if the very idea was absurd.

Maybe it didn't make sense, but Libera's expression was truthful. I couldn't help but believe her.

Hades, god of the dead, was here. Rumor called him rich and ruthless. Cold and terrifying. Stories never left out his piercing gray eyes, or the way even the other gods feared him. He was one god I'd never seen—about half of the other leaders had visited. What did he look like?

"I don't know why he's here," Libera shot back. "But Seph had better help me get ready for whatever he needs."

Mother focused on me. "I'm sure it's not actually Hades, darling. Just do whatever Libera says."

I pursed my lips. I would have done that anyway, since Libera was my supervisor. And part of me hoped it actually was Hades. His arrival would be the most exciting thing that had ever happened here. Another, more reasonable part of me didn't want the cruel god of the dead nearby. But lately I'd take excitement over routine if I could.

Just a look. I only wanted a look.

"Of course," I replied dutifully, giving Mother a nod to indicate it was okay for her to leave. I'd be all right. Libera wouldn't let anything happen to us if she could help it. And nothing would. Hades had no reason to harm a group of royal gardeners.

Libera didn't wait for Mother to latch the gate before dragging me closer to the palace through the maze of perfect hedges. The hard set to her face declared how annoyed she was at Mother, but Libera couldn't say anything against her without repercussions. After Vesta and the human queen who bore her name, Mother made the list of the most powerful beings in Kantharos.

"I don't know if he'll come out into the gardens, but we have to be ready if he does," she began in a rapid undertone.

My heart beat faster. "What do you need me to do?"

"You can check the worst flower beds and perk up their petals." She stopped to point at me. "No extra blooms. They're good as they are." Resuming her quick pace, she muttered the names of the flowers as though checking them off a mental list. "Phlox, primrose, geraniums..."

"I'll get them all," I assured her. "Don't worry." If I focused on the task, I could heal many wilting plants quickly.

"All right," she agreed, breathless. Her eyes had already slid away from me to other tasks.

I found I was breathless too. My skirt floated up behind me as I ran as quickly as I could, zigzagging through the meandering footpaths. Once, when I was younger, I'd jumped a hedge to get somewhere faster. The wrath I'd received for that almost made me cry.

I reached the primroses first. Leaning over the bush to the plot of flowers inside, I stroked the top of all the blossoms with my fingers. Sensing broken or dying flowers this way was like feeling for a snagged thread. Everything in its place and then—there! I made whatever little adjustments were necessary and then moved on to the delphiniums.

As I moved, I touched the trunks of the small trees scattered strategically around the large space. Might as well improve their health too. When every leaf in the garden bloomed with vibrant life, I had to admit it was breathtaking, despite how regimented everything was. Maybe even someone like Hades would—

Movement on the palace patio caught my attention. Someone was coming outside.

I sped up, casting a panicked look at Libera, who stood about halfway between me at the flagstone patio beyond, snipping at one of the hedge's fierce angles.

The door opened.

I moved so I could remain half-hidden behind a thin tree as I continued to work. Libera melted into the black morning shadows.

A man strode out first, utterly confident. Behind him followed the human queen. The enormous height of the male visitor—he dwarfed the queen—showed he was a god, but that wasn't the only clue. It was in every line of his body, the cut of his gaze, the authority that permeated everything about him.

He wore a dark, perfectly tailored suit that complemented his well-built frame. The fabric stretched slightly over his broad chest and arms before tapering to his waist. A dusting of beard highlighted the angle of his strong jaw, black hair over light skin. His piercing gray eyes swept over the garden in one intense sweep. He looked every bit a king surveying his territory.

I shivered. No wonder he was so feared. But why did no one talk about how gorgeous he was? It was almost painful to look at him. He was elegant and brutal—I could tell even from here. The air of threatening control only heightened his allure. My skin heated. He was like Dracon, someone built to seduce, to consume. I didn't think anyone could elicit such a strong reaction from me in real life. My response to his beauty frightened me as much as his presence here.

My hand had stopped exploring the tops of the flowers. If I didn't move, maybe he wouldn't see me. But I wasn't that far away, and as far as I could tell, I was the only gardener in his line of sight. What would I do if he...?

Those deep-set eyes locked onto mine. I felt a bolt run through me. Caught. I was caught.

The expanse of garden was so quiet between us that I heard the one clipped word he spoke to the queen. "Her."

❦ 4 ❦

HADES

The little goddess emerged from behind the square of hedges. Her eyes were huge, blue in a bronze face. Her yellow dress accentuated the smoothness of her skin with a belt cinching in the curve of her waist. The top part of the dress dipped down to show off her collarbone and a dark shadow of cleavage. Her powerful fingers remained mobile at her sides.

It was difficult to see from here, but this girl's power was reviving dead flowers. As I stared, I only caught her doing it once. A brown petal turned white just before we made eye contact.

She looked afraid. Made sense. It was rare for me to find a substantially different reaction from anyone meeting me for the first time.

I stepped back to assess her as she topped the shallow flight of stairs. Her chest trembled with shaky breathing. She looked extremely young, twenties maybe. Hopefully I hadn't come on a fool's errand. The Far Realm couldn't spare me.

"I have no further need of you," I told the human queen. Whether she was insulted, I didn't know, because I didn't watch her go.

I clasped my hands behind my back. "Persephone?"

"Seph."

I arched a brow.

"I prefer Seph, and everybody calls me that. But Persephone's fine too." She swallowed, her full mouth pursing as she did.

"What is your power, Seph?" I didn't like the nickname as much as her full name.

"I tend the plants in the palace garden here."

"That's your job. What is your power?" The information I'd gotten in Zenia had better be right. A minor goddess who had the power of life, the censor had said. The longer I looked at Persephone—Seph—the more I doubted she would last long in the Far Realm. It smelled tame here, floral. All these soft edges stirred something inside me I didn't like.

"I can revive flowers by touching them," she answered.

"Just flowers?"

"Other plants too. And insects." She looked almost ashamed at that.

"And," I prompted, sensing there was more.

"I can make new flowers grow too. I feel them in the earth and I just—"

"What about animals, people?"

"What?"

"Can you revive them?"

She cast a glance to the side, almost as if she were looking for someone, but we were completely alone.

"I've never tried," she finally answered.

My brows ticked down. She had the ability to revive living things and she'd *never tried?* I was wasting my time here. This girl was too young, too naïve, for what I wanted her to do.

It was time to go.

I got halfway across the flagstones before I halted and whirled back. Her dress did a pretty little thing as she twirled to meet my gaze again. Despite her ignorance of the harsher realities of life, she was alarmingly cute. Beautiful, even.

It was just that godsdamned ascension ceremony getting into my head. I hadn't taken time to unwind.

"Then it's time to try now," I said curtly, marching back to her. This was too important to abandon so quickly.

This time, I stood closer to her, close enough to smell the faint scent of strawberries wafting off her hair. Inside, the thing I kept leashed began to stir with excitement. Curling my lip in impatience, I held out my hand and sliced a line across the palm. It was always a good idea to keep a knife handy. You never knew when you'd need it.

Persephone gasped and covered her mouth. Her eyes flashed from my face to my bloody hand and back.

"Fix it," I ordered calmly.

"I don't know if I can—"

"Fix. It."

Her hands shook as she raised them, a concentrating line forming between her brows. "I... Normally, I have to touch the... the plants I'm healing. Is that all right?"

I almost smiled. I hadn't encountered innocence this profound in years. "Fine."

Her touch was soft, exploratory. Small fingers moved gently

over the skin of my palm, avoiding the welling blood. It was careful, whatever she was doing. I found myself enthralled with the designs she drew on me, feeling for... something. I didn't know how this kind of power worked, which is why I needed someone like her. If she could pass this test.

The pressure under her fingertips increased, and she closed her eyes. As though she didn't fully realize what she was doing, she brought her other hand up to cradle my calloused one so she could push down harder. Now she didn't avoid the blood anymore. She made spirals with it, new lines, and then she stroked the wound itself.

For the first time, the cut stung. When she made contact with it, my body reacted more strongly than it should have. My hand pulsed and danced with pinpricks. She rubbed the wound, almost petting it, her movements sensual and precise. She'd figured something out.

With one last stroke down the center, she exhaled and opened her eyes. The hand that hadn't been tracing my cut pulled away as if she'd been caught doing something wrong. My blood glazed her fingertips.

I wiped the thumb of my uninjured hand across my bloody palm. Under the red was smooth skin.

When we locked eyes again, hers were bright and uncertain. The hint of a smile played on her lips, though. Victory, it said. Pride.

I raised one side of my mouth in return. We were both breathing harder than we should have been. But this, *this*, could change everything.

PERSEPHONE

My heart thundered as I looked up at Hades' crooked smile. He held his hand in front of him, palm upward, filling the tiny space between us. My fingers still buzzed from the contact. I'd just massaged the god's hand, and he allowed it. The touch had felt forbidden, too intimate to be right. The pads of my fingers remembered the warm calluses on his palm. And the slice he'd made in the middle of it.

I healed him. I actually healed him.

Why had I never tried that before?

I caught my breath and rubbed my dirty fingers against each other. The sensation as he healed sizzled uncomfortably through my entire body, my power hugely magnified compared to the bits I parceled out to the plants and insects. But I couldn't deny the god of the dead. Now, I was glad he'd demanded it.

Hades stood rod-straight, so close I could smell the scent of night air clinging to him. His famous gray eyes were alight with intensity. My core began to ache and I clenched my thighs under my dress to halt the feeling.

"This is perfect," he said, plucking a handkerchief from a pocket and wiping the blood off his hand. The slight distance that movement created snapped the cord of tension I hadn't realized was building. "There's no need to gather your things. I'll provide anything you require once we're there. I need you in the Far Realm."

Stunned, I couldn't react. When I didn't say anything or move, he handed me the handkerchief. Mechanically, I rubbed my fingers clean and handed it back.

The reality of his words hit me like a slap. The Far Realm? With Hades? "I... I can't leave. My mother—"

"Can spare you, I'm sure," he replied quickly, not looking at me anymore. Instead, he paced a few steps away and looked toward the perfect hedge maze with an expression that said he saw none of it. He was considering logistics or something. All his movements had become business-like. I wasn't supposed to argue.

"They need me here too, Lord Hades," I said, fury rising as I planted my feet.

"I'll pay for two more gardeners." He waved his newly healed hand dismissively.

"I can't go to the Far Realm." Anger and fear threatened to choke me. This was happening too quickly. I couldn't think of what to do. What would Mother do? What would the character Esmeralda do in this situation? Oh, she was no help. She would enjoy being spirited off.

Finally, Hades returned his attention to me with a look of

vague irritation. "You can and you will. We need your services. I'm leaving now."

Should I scream? I was being kidnapped. But who could come to save me from a god who made the other gods quail?

Tears bit at the corners of my eyes. "Can I at least say goodbye?"

He gave a meaningful glance at the sun as if to note the time. "Would you like to know what my power is?" he asked, voice low.

"What is it?" Mine dropped too—almost a whisper. I hadn't thought to ask. It didn't seem proper with a god of his stature. Had I heard about his power before? I racked my brain. King Thenios had lightning... No, I didn't know it. Everything about Hades was shrouded in dread and mystery. He didn't even have a symbol like the other gods did. Death was everywhere and nowhere, Mother told me when I was memorizing the symbols as a child.

His jaw flexed. "When the sunlight hits this patio, we leave. Don't make me wait." That wasn't an answer, but it did sound like a threat.

I wanted to say goodbye to so many people, so many things. This had been my home my entire life. I'd never traveled off the island. And now Hades was ripping it away. No wonder Libera acted so panicky at his arrival. In a moment, he'd upended everything.

I could see the line of shadow move along the ground toward the stairs a fraction.

And I fled.

My yellow skirt floated behind me in my speed. Mother first. She had to know what was happening. By the time I reached the house, tears blinded me. I wrenched open the door. Hopefully she hadn't left for the fields yet. Judging by the light, it would be close.

The space smelled like baked bread. I raced to the kitchen and fell into Mother's arms.

Alarmed, she pushed me away from her so she could look in my face. "Persephone, what happened? What's the matter?"

For a few moments, I couldn't catch my breath.

"What?" she demanded, more harshly now.

"Hades. It was him," I panted. "He's really here. And... and now... he wants me to go with him."

Mother stiffened, her grip tightening on my shoulders. Ferocity shone in her eyes. "Go with him? But you can't."

"I have to. He's leaving in a minute."

"Why does he want you?"

"My power, I think."

"That doesn't make any sense, Seph." Her gaze flickered down to my neckline, which had dropped since this morning, before rising to meet mine again.

"No, Mother," I said, exasperated. Mother always assumed men, deathless or not, had designs on me. It was ludicrous. None ever had. Certainly not the infamous god of the dead. "It's my power. He thinks it will help him somehow."

"I'll tell him it won't." Bread forgotten, Mother marched out of the house.

Feeble protests bubbled up in my throat but I didn't get them out as I followed her. My chest warmed with tiny hope at having someone who loved me enough to defend me. I had no idea what Mother could do against Lord Hades, but I wanted to find out. As long as his mysterious power didn't hurt her...

"Wait!" I cried, tugging her back.

"Seph, let go!"

"No. I think he'll hurt you if you try to stop him."

Mother laid her hand on the garden gate latch, just as she'd done mere minutes ago before my world tipped over and broke. "I'm just going to talk sense into him."

That sounded reasonable. I released my death-grip on her arm, but my pulse still charged so fiercely through my chest that it hurt. The argument for staying felt simple. Maybe even the god of death would understand. Even as I thought it, I fought against despair. What Hades wanted, he got. And right now, he wanted me.

When Mother reached the shaded patio where Hades stood insolently leaning against the palace wall, she swept to one knee. "My lord."

He regarded her as someone would regard something a little disgusting.

Mother rose from her bow before I realized I was supposed to kneel too. Everything was happening too fast. I couldn't keep up. Sunlight had reached the top step. I gripped the folds of my skirt in white-knuckled fists to keep from wringing my hands.

"What's this?" Hades didn't so much as push away from the wall.

"We met, my lord, a long time ago. My name is Demeter," Mother explained.

His only reaction was the barest quirk of a brow.

"My daughter tells me you want her to go with you. She cannot do that today."

His sculpted mouth betrayed amusement and annoyance

before he locked eyes with me. "Are you finished with good-byes, then?"

"Lord Hades," Mother tried again, more desperate now. There was a challenge in her angry stare. I admired her for the courage it took to stand up to this god, but it wouldn't do any good. Mother was a full goddess, but nothing compared to Hades.

"Persephone," he said in a clear voice, finally straightening. His narrowed gaze fell to the light climbing the final step. "It's time to go."

"You can't take her."

The icy look he directed at Mother sent my skin tingling with fear. His eyes darkened almost to black.

My feet moved before I could think. "No, I'll go."

Mother wheeled on me. "Seph!" she scolded, but the lines on her forehead showed how worried she was.

Mouth dry, I passed her and trudged up the steps. "I'll be okay." The words came out as no more than a breath. Did I even believe them?

Hades waited for me, the picture of cruel poise. When I stood before him, he extended his arm. The back of my neck prickled.

A beat of hesitation, then I laid my hand on his forearm.

"No, Seph, don't!"

Mother's desperate cry followed me into the darkness as Hades and I disappeared.

My entire torso felt squeezed by a massive snake as Hades stepped through the air to take me to the Far Realm. I'd traveled this way before—all gods and demi-gods could do it—but never this far. I couldn't breathe. Darkness and space folded around me, closing me in. Panic crawled up my throat and then...

We landed. I was hanging onto something. With a start, I realized it was Hades. I didn't just have my hand on his fore-arm, but I had wrapped my arms around his middle like a squirrel clinging to a tree. My knees wobbled with the intensity of the trip, but Hades didn't so much as waver.

I released my hold, blinking around. We stood in a temple-style building with tall columns, except that it wasn't open to the sky as most temples were. Stone walls enclosed everything. The inside was so dark and hot it might have been underground.

Beside one of many burning braziers arranged in a ring, a

man and two women whirled at our entrance. They instantly fell on their faces.

Hades cracked his neck and rolled his shoulders, hardly seeming to care about the prostrate worshippers.

"My king," cried the man without lifting his head, "what word from the dead?"

"No word," came Hades' response.

I gave him a questioning look. Was this the Far Realm? Why had we appeared here, and what was I supposed to do?

His gaze slanted sideways to me. Was I supposed to bow too?

"It's too far to travel all the way," he explained to me quietly. "This is on the Bridge."

The Bridge connected the war-torn country of Eriset with King Lox's peaceful domain of Hyperion. Just a skinny bit of shoreline that looked like nothing on a map.

We'd have to make another jump. Home was already far away. Another distance like the one we'd already crossed felt like something I could never come back from. I'd be completely adrift in a strange land, far from anything I knew. That knowledge and the heat of the dark flames made me lightheaded.

"How may we serve you, my lord?" asked one of the women.

All three humans wore black robes despite the heat. I got the feeling that they waited in this chamber for this exact possibility—that Hades would appear.

The god, on the other hand, barely acknowledged their existence. He waved a hand. "I require nothing."

He took a couple deep, deliberate breaths, almost like a swimmer. Firelight glinted on his black hair as he turned again to me. Every time he fixed his attention on me, I felt trapped. His attention burned like something physical. "And again," he said simply. "Hold on if you prefer." There was a hint of derision in his curve of his mouth as he held out his arm once more.

Under the fine fabric of his sleeve, his muscles tensed.

I inhaled sharply and closed my eyes.

Distance crushed around us like a smothering fist. This time it took even longer. By the time we arrived and space snapped into normal dimensions, I was shaking. I'd managed not to hug Hades' waist, but my two-handed grip on his arm would probably leave bruises. I pried my fingers off him, gasping, barely strong enough to stand.

It was cold. My arms, neck, and ankles, not covered by my flowing dress, instantly cooled. Trying to gather my wits, I looked around again. This time, we weren't in some creepy underground temple. We stood in a dim, high-roofed hall made of blue-gray marble. It made me think of vampire castles I'd read about.

Beside me, Hades lifted his chin and adjusted his suit before striding off down the hall. I tripped after him. My weak legs didn't like the pace he chose. On him, it didn't look fast, but his legs were longer than mine, so I had to jog to keep up. All the deathless were tall compared to humans, but there weren't any humans around now. Hades towered over me, made me feel small.

"Is this... is this the Far Realm?" I huffed. Windows flew past too quickly to see much. A flash of pines on the left, black waves on the right.

"This is it." His tone was low and measured. I couldn't tell if he was proud or disappointed. Maybe just distracted. He acted like he was too busy to look my way.

Anger rekindled inside me. He'd just kidnapped me and now he wouldn't even acknowledge my presence?

"Lord Hades," I said, more loudly now, "please, at least tell me what you want me to do."

"I want you to help the dead."

Before I could react, a figure glided toward us. She wore a long, gauzy white gown a shade paler than her skin and a head-dress of antlers. Her lips had been painted black. Somehow, even with red around her eyes and a creepy ghostliness about her, she was beautiful.

I felt too conspicuous as the only bit of color in the huge room. Strangely, standing next to Hades, who acted so competent in these weird surroundings, made me a little less afraid.

"Welcome back, my lord," the figure said, her voice very low for a female. "Who is this?" She pointed one long black fingernail at me.

I tensed.

"Someone to help at the wharf. Retrieval," Hades answered. "Her name is Persephone. Once you help her get settled, take her to learn her duties. Give her anything she wants." He left my side without another word.

"Wait." I couldn't help it. The word was out before I knew what I was doing. "You're just going to leave me here?"

"Did you think I'd show you everything myself?" When he put it that way, it sounded foolish. The king of the Far Realm personally attending to my needs... I really had read too many books.

But the thought of him abandoning me with this ghostly woman, whose name I didn't even know, turned my stomach. What else lurked here?

I didn't have a chance to answer before his shoes tapped a steady rhythm and his back retreated, finally disappearing around a corner.

Help with the dead. What did that mean? I trembled, partly from fear and partly from cold.

"Persephone?" the ghost-woman said, cocking her head like a bird of prey would before shrieking down upon its dinner.

"Seph, please," I managed.

Her black lips turned upward. "Let's get you to your room."

THE ROOM WAS... GORGEOUS. AND IT SMELLED LIKE HADES, like fresh night air. Everything about it was like him, commanding with strong lines and obvious wealth. The only difference was how comfortable it made me feel.

Thick, sumptuous rugs covered the floor with dark patterns. The four-poster bed fluffed with many blankets and pillows. Since it was so chilly, I wanted to dive into them.

Kantharos stayed temperate all the time. In the depth of winter, the garden sometimes experienced one frost. Libera had us cover all the plants just in case.

Here, all was frozen elegance. Sconces attached to the walls made me think of ice sculptures, even though they were black. Two of them flanked a tall, thin window that looked out to a churning ocean. The Stygian Sea. I'd heard of it but never seen it for myself. It looked savage and beautiful, its black waves cresting white in the stormy, wet moonlight.

I turned from the view back to the ghostly, antler-crested woman who had guided me here.

"Will this suit you?" she asked.

"This is just for me? No other... workers?" My awe fractured when I remembered I was still little more than a prisoner here. At least I would be a stylish prisoner.

"No." That creepy, evaluating look came over her again. Vampires had come to mind earlier. Was she one of them?

"What's your name?" I asked.

"Marzanna." It was a good, earthy name. I suddenly missed my books. Hades hadn't given me time to plunder my cozy hidden shed.

"That's a pretty name."

A smile spread over her black lips. I smiled back. No use alienating anybody who was nice to me.

I trailed my fingertips over an austere little table in front of the window. "What do you do for Lord Hades?"

"Whatever he needs." Her deep voice held surprising conviction. What did that mean? "Do you need anything else from me, Seph?"

My name sounded odd in her mouth. And the question sounded even weirder. No one had ever asked me that before.

"No," I answered automatically. This room was already nicer than any place I'd had to myself before, and Mother was a full goddess whose cottage rivaled any house.

Then I remembered I had no clothes, no soap, no flowers, nothing.

"Very well," said Marzanna. "If you require no more time to prepare yourself, then Lord Hades said he needs you at the wharf."

To help the dead. Worry lodged in my throat.

Seeing the bedroom, like something out of a winter fairy tale, had almost made this predicament feel like a fun adventure. Now the reality clawed at me. This wasn't fun. It wasn't the escape I'd longed for. Hades required my services to somehow help him with the dead. If I didn't, strict consequences would probably follow.

As I followed Marzanna obediently out of the room and through the castle—this had to be Hades' castle—I ran through what I knew about Hades' dealings with the human dead.

Corpses could be sent to the Far Realm on little boats if you paid for passage.

The cost was two gold coins, one for each eye.

Humans talked about experiencing another life here, some kind of afterlife.

No one agreed if it was good or bad, only that they couldn't return.

That was it. All I knew. If I was sent to the wharf, that had to be the place where the dead bodies were dropped off. I fought off a gag. I was a gardener, not an undertaker. Demigods didn't die like humans did. I hated to see decay even in moths. What would I do if I had to look at a dead human?

Fur swept over my bare arm and I flinched back. A rumble that might have been a laugh echoed through Marzanna. She held a thick coat out to me.

"Where did you get this?" I asked, taking it gratefully. I sensed we were getting close to exterior doors.

She didn't answer.

As soon as I wrapped the coat around myself, a blast of frigid air blew my hair back. I squinted against it. Wetness flew on the wind, coating my face. Shivering, I cracked my eyes open enough to see Marzanna step placidly down a long, narrow set of stone stairs that hugged one wall of the great castle. There wasn't even a handrail to guard from the sheer drop on the other side. What if the steps were icy? I gripped the coat, which fell to my knees, and trundled down as carefully as I could.

Waves crashed nearby so I assumed we were heading to the shore, but I kept my attention on the next stair, always the next stair. Marzanna must not have been bothered by the frozen storm because she didn't so much as cross her arms. I imagined her antler crown blowing off and impaling me in the face. After the day I'd had, anything seemed possible.

When we finally reached the bottom, I was shaking so violently that my teeth clacked together. My dainty shoes squished into wet sand. Those were my favorite shoes, and now the only ones I owned. But I had no choice; I had to trudge forward. Who knew what they would do if I fell behind. I doubted Hades would coddle me. I placed my feet in the footprints left by Marzanna. Sea salt mixed with something rancid on the air. I wrinkled my nose, hating each step more.

I yelped as I ran into Marzanna's back, the sound drowned by the wind. She had stopped. We'd arrived. I let go of the coat with one freezing hand and wiped the plastered hair out of my eyes.

And screamed.

PERSEPHONE

A creature towered over me. That wasn't unusual, but this one towered over Marzanna as well. It rose up on a muscular snake body that could have kept going and going. I couldn't even see the end of the thick, scaly coils. The lashing wind and rain washed the slithering flesh muddy gray. The snake-like body melted into human skin at the navel. A female figure commandeered that monstrous body, thick but ultimately feminine, with strong, graceful arms and round, naked breasts. Her face was ageless, not in the way of the deathless, but more ancient, more primal. Her large, dark eyes had seen a thousand lifetimes, had killed and birthed hundreds, and feared nothing.

Her attention fell on me.

"Screaming," she said quietly, barely audible over the storm. When the creature's focus shifted to Marzanna, I released a shaky breath. "What have you brought me, Marzanna?" I never would have guessed her voice. At least, I'd never heard anything like it. The words came out soft, like the sound of the ocean was soft, each sound given its due. I felt as though, when she said them, the words were completely new. Had I ever heard someone say the word *screaming* before?

"This is Seph," Marzanna answered, unfazed by this monster. "Lord Hades says she's here to help you at the wharf."

"Much to do," came that alien voice again. The sinuous body slithered even closer.

I held my breath.

The weather didn't seem to bother her as she scrutinized me. Rain streamed from her frayed black hair—somehow still lovely, as if it had grown on her like moss. I hardly felt the elements anymore either. The force of this creature had stolen every other sensation. It was like when Hades locked eyes with me in the garden. His gaze trapped me, sent a jolt through my body that set me alight with anticipation and the certainty that I didn't deserve his attention.

I felt trapped now too. The smell of decay wafted powerfully through the air. I was supposed to help this creature? How in the Eight Realms was I supposed to accomplish that?

"What is your power?" The unearthly head canted to one side.

"I..." My voice sounded pitifully thin next to hers. "I can make plants grow." I couldn't catch my breath. "And insects, I can heal them. I healed Lord Hades when he asked me to."

"Healed Lord Hades."

"He had a cut and... he asked me to fix it." The memory of my fingers dragging along his calloused palm flooded me with enough heat that I felt more comfortable in the stinking cold.

The head canted to the other side with the hypnotic movement of a snake. I tensed. Would she strike? There was nowhere I could run, nowhere to escape...

"You shall help," the snake woman said slowly. Was that... Did she look *pleased*? It was difficult to tell. Just a relaxing of some facial muscles, a blink.

My heart still pounded, but I was proud of myself for having stood my ground. Being whisked away from the life I knew, told to work in the freezing cold, and meeting several new and frankly scary beings hadn't harmed me so far. Naïve as I knew it was, that knowledge gave me courage.

"What's your name?" I asked.

At my question, the snake-creature smiled, or at least stretched her lips to show her teeth. "All know my name."

"I don't. Yet."

From the corner of my eye, Marzanna's antlers swiveled toward me. Had I been too bold? Well, it was too late now.

Just like Esmeralda. Just pretend it's a story. You'll be all right, I chanted to myself.

"Drakaina," the creature hissed.

She was right. I had heard the name. She was the Mother, the mate of Typhon, one of the First Beings, an eater of flesh. I grew up on stories of her.

So the rumors about the Far Realm were true. It did crawl with monsters.

"Come," she said imperiously, shifting her massive, scaly body. "There are new arrivals all the time."

To my surprise, Marzanna followed too. I had thought she worked directly for Hades or something. Maybe a personal servant, based on the way she greeted us when we arrived.

These beings were like two sides of death—Marzanna was

weird and ethereal, something seen out of the corner of the eye in deep woods, and Drakaina was ancient and solid and unavoidable. I blinked against the driving rain and followed them up the coast. Drakaina's snake body was so long I could barely see the end.

Salty waves crashed, wild and dangerous, to our right. The spray caught me with a shocking chill more than once. I was sopping, and the smell wasn't getting better either. Part of the odor came from Drakaina. My stomach twisted with horrible guesses about the reason.

Soon, shouts cut through the dark storm. Workers struggling with something. Next, a wharf appeared, slick and black, extending far out into the roiling surf. My breathing shortened. Would I have to go out on that dangerous little path through the ocean?

Small figures wrestled with ropes attached to small boats bobbing like toys in the water. Others seemed to be carrying heavy loads and placing them in a pile in the opposite direction from us. People periodically approached one male, a leader of some kind, who held a box. The final group moved among the discarded loads carrying long poles. At the top of each pole was a lantern and below that, attached horizontally just above the head of each moving figure, was a cylindrical object.

The whole scene became clearer through the murk as we drew closer. The small boats held one or two dead humans each. I doubted this was what humans pictured when they sent their loved ones across the Stygian Sea for a chance at an afterlife. Those hauling them in were a motley group—demi-gods, probably, judging from the wide variety in body structure. Demi-gods didn't need to look humanoid, and some of these certainly didn't fit that mold, although their eyes held intelligence. A wolfish creature with hair matted down by the stormy rain slanted a look at me as we approached.

"Take this."

I whipped around to see Marzanna holding out a pair of shears she hadn't been holding before. My mind flashed to Libera. Did she know what happened to me? At least she hadn't been stolen to help in the war in Eriset. Right now, though, my predicament didn't seem any better.

Shakily, I took the shears. What was I supposed to do with these?

Drakaina didn't introduce me. I wished she had, so the wolfish creature and the others—a bat man and huge, scaly lizard walking upright—would know not to threaten me. They wouldn't hurt me... Would they? If Hades told them not to touch me, they'd stay away. Too bad he'd disappeared as soon as we arrived. Kidnapping was just another day for him, apparently.

I tightened my fingers around the frigid metal handle of the shears. Fighting off a shiver, I said, "What do you want me to do?"

Drakaina slithered past Marzanna, who stayed behind to organize something related to the boats, and I followed. We headed toward the pile of cargo.

Or...

Wait. Not cargo.

These were dead bodies. Gorge rose up in my throat, but I forced it down. Hundreds of bodies thrown carelessly on top of each other. Some looked like they were sleeping, and others had wounds so terrible I could barely recognize them as human. More demi-gods picked their way through the carnage with their lantern poles, singing. All their songs clashed and blended maddeningly with each other, audible above the roar of wind and waves, but only just. I strained to hear, but I'd lose one thread only to grasp onto another...

"You healed Hades," came Drakaina's powerful voice.

My pulse galloped. I healed a little cut. I couldn't raise the dead.

I didn't reply.

"You will help here. Too many souls are lost. We do not have enough vessels to capture them, and the bodies are too much for me to handle on my own. Hades wishes for more humans to experience a second life. So, for those humans who are not greatly damaged, attempt to heal them. The Singers will teach you the song. If any are beyond your skill"—her serpent eyes flicked down to the shears in my hand—"you will cut a lock of hair and feed it to the flame."

I could barely keep up with what she was saying. I opened my mouth to protest, ask questions, *something*, but she had already slid away.

The stench almost made me keel over, but I fought to keep my attention sharp. When the first Singer approached with his lantern pole, I called out, "Please, I don't what I'm supposed to do. I can't heal the dead. I'm just a... just a gardener."

He approached carefully, stepping over the bodies. This being looked human, like a young man in the prime of life, except for how pale he was. He wore a heavy raincoat and his deep-set eyes glittered, not as brightly as Hades' but there was a small similarity. He too carried scissors.

"Hello," he greeted, with far more cheer than I would have expected. "Are you lost?"

"No," I said, frowning. I brandished the scissors. "Hades brought me here to help, but Drakaina's instructions... I didn't understand them at all." Slashing rain hid the tears that bit the corners of my eyes. And I'd been here less than two hours. *You can do this, Seph.* I sniffed in a fortifying breath and immediately wished I hadn't.

The young man smiled ruefully. "She can be hard to follow sometimes. Here." He offered his hand.

I stared at it. Did he expect me to climb up there with him?

Someone threw down another corpse near my feet. I jumped, taking the young man's hand and stepping up. Light from the lantern threw a faint glow on our faces. Being able to see more clearly was a small comfort in this dreadful situation.

If only I could snuggle up with a cup of tea and a book by a warm fireplace...

"I'm Tos," he said.

"Seph."

"I'm surprised they didn't give you a pole. We're very busy in this section."

"They just gave me these." I waved the shears again. "Drakaina said something about songs and hair and healing people."

"You can heal people?" A strange light entered his eyes, which were remarkably light to match the rest of him.

"I... not..."

"If you can heal bodies, that would be tremendous! Most humans, if we can catch their spirits in time, have to live just like that—as spirits. But if you can transform their bodies into something that could house their souls again, maybe some would get an afterlife with their original body, which would help us out a lot." He spoke cheerfully but very quickly. "We have many unused bodies as it is. And we can only catch so many souls at once before they dissipate and there's no chance of helping them."

"What about the scissors?"

Tos bent down and clipped a lock of hair from a dead woman near where we stood, lowered the pole, and dropped the hair into the open top of the lantern. The smell of burning hair joined the scent of decay. I covered my nose and mouth with one hand.

His smile widened at my expression. "It's not glamorous, I know."

A bluish, white vapor ribboned from the woman to the cylinder. With the storm, I couldn't be perfectly sure of what I'd seen, but it definitely looked like *something*.

"Yeah," said Tos. "We're their chance for an afterlife." His expression grew serious and thoughtful.

My brow furrowed. There was still so much I didn't begin to understand, and so much that disturbed me about this whole process, but I came here to assist these dead humans. If I didn't help, all my pain today would be for nothing. So I nodded at Tos and got to work.

❧ 8 ❧

PERSEPHONE

The victim lay clammy and rigid under my fingertips, but not greatly injured. This was nothing like digging my hands in the rich soil of the queen's garden and sensing tendrils of life. Here, there was no life. Just cold, gummy flesh. I was losing my battle against nausea.

Closing my eyes, I focused on reaching my energy deeper. Flowers were easy. Insects took a little more focus. This task meant skipping over so many levels to my ability that I hadn't mastered—assuming those levels existed. Deathless abilities were either unique or very rare, so every person had to figure them out for themselves. I couldn't count on help.

I felt the body's core, still the slightest bit warm despite the lashing rain. Maybe that was something, though I still felt sick. The thought of my bare calves nearly touching this body...

Focus. Focus.

This was more than a body. It had been a person, a young woman with light skin, long dark hair, freckles, and a crooked nose. Lines around her thin mouth revealed that she was quick to smile or frown. She lived a complex life before it was cut short. She had a name too.

Her insides cooled as quickly as I sensed them. This blasted storm! Helplessness threatened to overtake me. Back home, I wasn't exactly what they needed—not orderly enough, not focused enough—and here, with much more at stake, those flaws were laid bare in the worst way. If I couldn't heal this woman somehow, or knit her back together, or *something*, then her spirit would evaporate without ever being recovered for an afterlife.

With a frustrated groan, I opened my eyes to search among the bodies. So many bodies... "Tos! I can't... I need you to come here."

Pursing my lips tight against the lump in my throat, I lifted a lock of the woman's dark hair and snipped it off. If I put it in Tos's lantern and he sang the song, which they still hadn't taught me, then she could still be reclaimed.

He didn't respond.

"Tos!"

Finally, he turned, still a long way away. "Yes, Seph?" he called back.

Another worker, this one with bull-like features over a mannish torso and legs, looked at us curiously.

"It's not working." I tried to keep my voice steady. I held up the lock of hair drooping with the weight of rain. Sadness and shame threatened to drown me.

"My cylinder's full after this one! Try again." His tone wasn't cruel, but the reality of his words hurt so horribly that I nearly clutched my stomach.

"You?" I asked the bull-headed worker, stumbling to my

feet. Maybe if I got there fast enough, I could throw the hair in the flame and...

He shook his head and moved away from me.

"Just try again," Tos urged. In the light from his lantern, still miraculously flickering in the storm, he looked sympathetic. "Try your best, but we always lose a lot of them."

The revelation numbed me, made me waver on my feet as I picked my way back to the young woman. No one could help me? But I had no training, I wasn't prepared, and now this woman's eternity rested on my shoulders.

Desperately, I flung myself on the body once I found it again. I felt the nearby dead like a weight pressing down harder and harder on my chest. It wasn't only one woman, but hundreds and hundreds.

Summoning whatever focus I had, I cupped the woman's face. This time, I didn't wince at the feel of her skin. She had hobbies and lovers and deserved to find a second chance here.

I would give it to her.

"Come on," I whispered, imagining she was a garden plot. My energy searched insistently, feeling for anything to hold onto. Nothing, nothing, nothing.

Then, something.

I grasped it, holding my breath until I drew it out.

At the woman's temple, between my fingers, grew a small white flower.

I doubled over with sobs.

By the time Marzanna fetched me back to the castle, my limbs were stiff as death with cold. I'd tried to revive seven more humans. I'd managed to catch the spirit of one, but only after cutting his hair and finding an available lantern—a seemingly impossible task. I still didn't know the song they all sang. I was too focused on my failing attempts to somehow bring humans back from the dead.

Maybe it's better for spirits to disappear instead of existing here forever.

The chilly castle felt warm compared to outside. Ever since I arrived, the storm made everything as dark as night, so I had no idea what time it was. It felt like nightmare days had passed.

Marzanna's diaphanous dress dried suspiciously quickly in the castle. I followed her antlered head numbly. Here, wind and rain couldn't drown out my crying.

Once we reached the room she'd shown me earlier, I faced Marzanna. She appeared completely calm, as if what I'd just experienced wasn't out of the ordinary. Personally, meeting flesh-eating primal snake goddesses and *losing* the souls of innocent humans wasn't something I could get used to.

"Will Lord Hades send me back?" I asked. The words came out small and hoarse.

Marzanna tilted her head. "Why would he send you back?"

My brows lowered. "Because I couldn't do what he asked."

"Any help is welcome."

I glanced out the thin window flanked by black ice sconces to the sea. Even now, with any sleep I got, more souls would disappear. The responsibility was crushing.

"I can't... do what you want," I pleaded, feeling new tears well up. I was so tired, and this was too much. I felt terrible for the dead, but what could I do to help? If anything, I'd get in the way.

My heart beat in my throat. Visions of Mother and our house and the royal garden struck like a blow. "I wish I could," I went on.

Marzanna raised one ghostly, long-nailed hand to stop me. "If Lord Hades brought you here, he had a reason. What can I get you this evening?"

She wasn't listening. I didn't have the powers he thought I did. "Nothing," I said bitterly.

"Nothing at all?" Her head tilted the other way. "We have steamed puddings and scented soaps. Dry clothes."

Any luxury felt selfish, but I couldn't help answering, "Dry clothes, please."

Marzanna flourished a hand, looked me up and down, and grasped something out of the air. It was a long purple nightgown.

I sucked in a breath. I'd never seen power like that. "Did you... just make that?"

Her black lips curved. "I summon. I don't make." She set the nightgown on the bed and repeated the motion to produce a fluffy gray robe.

Just seeing them made me moan with appreciation. "Thank you." I took the robe from her and hugged it to my chest, not caring that it got damp.

"Do you require anything else?"

"No."

"Then you may rest." She said it as though she never rested herself. "I advise you not to leave your room until I come to wake you in the morning. We provide refuge for many discarded beings. Some would be harmful to you if you encountered them in the night. And don't under any circumstances travel west into the woods."

I quirked a brow, curiosity rising despite my bone-deep exhaustion. "What's in the woods?"

"Much of the Far Realm," she said strangely. "And some places it were better to die than to discover."

Unease crawled up my spine. I didn't push the issue.

"'Til the morning," she declared, drifting back to the door.

I waved goodbye, still clutching the robe. Once the door shut tight, leaving me inside, I released a heaving breath. Flames flickered in the sconces. I inhaled the fresh scent of the dry clothes. So much of my night had been death and decay. These clothes smelled like fresh snow under a star-strewn sky. Dark but peaceful.

With a burst of resolve, I charged toward the window. Placing my hand on the cold sill, I drew on my power and a lovely pink bloom blossomed through cracks in the stone. My forehead scrunched as I stared at it, tension ebbing from my body.

A minute passed like that before I finally stripped off my sopping dress and put on the nightclothes. Then I crawled beneath the soft sheets with robe and all. Sleep took me as surely as the grave.

I glared at the wooden model laid out before me and frowned. This wasn't good. In my brief absence to attend the Eclipse Ceremony in Zenia before picking up Persephone, even more threads had unraveled here. Dock collectors failed to distribute the earnings correctly, more space needed to be cultivated for human bodies and spirits, and the protective measures I'd imposed on Abaddon were wearing thin.

There were too many urgent problems and not enough solutions. For the god-prison, I'd starting learning the most difficult fucking language in the kingdom—Qa-a-ka. My tutor had just stepped out. A new language meant new ideas, new connections, and new protective wards I could summon to keep the criminal gods in check. Plus, I could understand trolls. Best to be able to communicate with as many subjects as possible. Even if I loathed my lessons in this particular tongue.

Now, for the humans...

I tapped some trees on the interactive map, envisioning an expansion to the hilly region where many of the human spirits dwelled. But those trees were sacred to a faction of nymphs who had lived on this land almost as long as I had. In my youth, I had the devil of a time finding them a suitable place to live. Their current situation fit them perfectly. I couldn't destroy the trees.

Destruction seemed to be half my job—whether that meant destroying empty bodies or my own reputation—but I usually avoided it when I could.

I squinted at the fuller map on the wall, one of the only complete maps of the Far Realm in existence. Most maps only showed the southeastern tip. Further inland, it grew wild. At its heart lived evil things, many of which I'd met and befriended on the condition that we leave each other alone for the most part. On the western bank, where my brothers didn't dare to explore, I had many lucrative ventures and even thriving cities. Demi-gods and human spirits from the distant past worked side by side to provide food, weapons, and building materials for the kingdom.

We were self-sufficient here in the Far Realm. More than that. Between the industry on the west coast and the business of collecting bodies on the east, I had more money than I knew what to do with. The only reason I exacted the two-coin toll at all was to slow the influx of more human bodies into my already congested docks. Few had the ability to harvest souls or dispose of bodies—Drakaina was most efficient.

Most "monsters" made incredibly good allies, if you gave them what they wanted—human flesh, solitude, a place to call home.

I didn't see an obvious place to expand the human lands. My problem was one of labor. Despite having enough funds to build additional cities, I had to think of all those who would have to stop their jobs to construct them, if they even knew how. I couldn't spare a single person at the docks. The best work force would be the human spirits, but I wouldn't compel them to work for me. They'd already died, for gods' sake. The least I could give them was a little peace, if they wanted it.

After centuries of work and piles of treasure, I had only achieved a barely functioning ecosystem that this endless war between the Twins was throwing out of balance. Too many humans were dying. Hopefully Persephone—sweet, innocent Persephone, poor thing—could help the dire situation at the over-crowded docks.

The memory of her soft hand holding mine, painting swirls of blood on my palm, sent an ache low in my gut. She smelled like strawberries and spring. She had eternity ahead of her and a gift that could help thousands. I'd been entirely justified in recruiting her. But maybe she wouldn't survive her first day here without crippling trauma. The idea soured my mood even more.

What choice did I have? Persephone was capable. I needed her. But there wasn't a lot of innocence left in the Far Realm. I hated to think that her experience here would stifle that earnest, fresh way about her.

I groaned and raked my fingers through my hair. I had everything. Why did it feel like I was one bad day from every-thing falling apart?

A whisp of white at the door announced Marzanna's arrival. I pushed my black hair back into place and straightened. She casually took in the model, the bookcases, the desk, the tall, dark blue drapes, the map on the wall, and the meticulously stacked papers on my desk.

"The collector is here, as you requested," she said.

I adjusted my cuffs, took a breath. "And it's confirmed?"

"His misconduct? Yes, my lord."

I sighed. Everyone knew not to cross me. I ran the Far Realm as generously as I dared, but beyond that, there sliced a sharp line. Anyone who chose to step over it would not know my mercy.

"Bring him in."

"Yes, my lord."

The dock collector trembled as he entered. He was a demigod named Selig whom I'd given sanctuary to after his own kingdom tried to kill him as an abomination, just because of his fire-red eyes. The rest of his aspect looked human enough, maybe a little angular in the jaw or long in the fingers.

"Selig," I purred in greeting.

His trembling intensified and he made no move closer. So I stalked closer to him. The smell of fear cut through the putrid sea-and-corpse scent that always accompanied those who had worked long at the docks. Claws knocked against the inside of my ribcage, my power begging to get out. I loosened its leash.

"Those tolls were for my workers, the ones who deal directly with the dead. It's a nasty business until the spirits are free. Wouldn't you agree, Marzanna?"

She offered a solemn, unconcerned nod.

I clasped my hands behind my back as I circled my prey. "Rewarding work, but much harder than holding a box. So, when I find out that one of my collectors thought he could take more for himself..."

A shadowy form solidified behind Selig. He caught it out of the corner of his eye and shifted his weight as if to run.

"Ah ah ah," I sang. "He is faster. *I* am faster." My smirk melted away into a raging glare. I stepped close enough that we almost touched. His chattering teeth set my own bones on edge. At least he understood what was coming. "You steal from me, you fucking bastard, and I steal from you."

The shadow fully materialized into a charcoal black version of myself, slightly fuzzy at the edges, but fully capable of force. I released my frustration into the other self, hardly seeing what method he used to hurt the man. Selig screamed and writhed before crumpling to the ground, pieces missing.

"Make sure the blood doesn't stain," I muttered, turning. A chill ran through me as the shadow self reabsorbed into my body. I had no time for this, for any of it.

Leaning against the desk, I took a steadying breath. "See if Evard can find a new collector to replace him."

"Of course, my lord."

"After you deliver that message, you're dismissed until tomorrow."

Marzanna never slept. In my mind, she had two divine abilities: summoning and perpetual wakefulness. She was the only one outside the prison of Abaddon who occasionally frightened me. That she chose to serve me was baffling sometimes. Dock work was thankless. The least I could do was give her occasional times to rest. Hopefully, that appeased her, if she did have some dark motive for helping me. I pictured her in a coffin or perhaps acting as a statue to scare passersby. I didn't ask for the truth.

"Persephone, the new arrival?"

I spun. "What about her?"

"You said she heals."

"She does."

"She can't."

I frowned, pinning Marzanna's red-rimmed eyes with my stare. "I saw her do it. I *felt* her do it."

"But she is unable to heal the bodies of the dead to recapture their spirits."

"Impossible."

Marzanna didn't repeat herself, but I felt her words echo through the vaulted space between us, where Selig still sprawled.

"That's why I brought her," I said. My detour to Kantharos had to pay off. Too many spirits were being lost. Better to make room for thousands more if I could.

Those were rational thoughts, but an urgent, irrational panic at the idea of sending her back also flashed through my veins. My sides remembered the way she'd held onto me so tightly as we traveled through the air. Few in the Far Realm ever touched me, even innocently, and she'd done it multiple times.

"Make her try again."

10

PERSEPHONE

I'd been in the Far Realm a week—a bloody, filthy week—and I couldn't stand it anymore. No one talked to me but Marzanna and Drakaina, who were both monstrous and aloof. I ached for home like I'd ached for nothing else in my whole life. I just wanted Mother to hold me and tell me I wasn't a failure.

But I was. I'd let dozens of human souls slip through my fingers and I couldn't help but grieve for each one. The pain obscured my ability to focus on the next body, and so on and so on. I'd finally learned the song and placed a few hairs in the lanterns, but those were usually too full to accommodate my souls as well. For each human I failed, I crowned them in flowers. It was silly. They couldn't enjoy it, but at least it made them more beautiful than the wrecks they had become.

The arch around my window grew wild with flowers by now. On nights when I didn't immediately curl into a tiny ball to attempt to fall asleep, I released some of my horrible tension by blooming plants in my room. I could hardly see out the tall window now. Pink and blue and white blossoms tangled around the sill and between the stones.

Hades never came to see me. Why did I think he would? Maybe the way he'd pierced his hand in the royal garden and ordered me to fix it or the way we'd journeyed together farther than I'd ever gone made me think so. But that was silly too. He was king of the dead and I couldn't even accomplish the job he'd kidnapped me to do. He didn't seem the type to stop by and chat.

I ran my finger around the rim of the gold platter that sat on my bed. On it was a warm loaf of bread and a pat of flavored butter with little bowls of optional toppings. I'd only asked Marzanna for a snack.

Everyone here treated me kindly, even Drakaina in her alien way. *I* was the problem. I couldn't help the humans, I couldn't feel thankful for all my hosts given me, and I couldn't rid myself of the feeling that maybe Hades himself might help somehow if he weren't so busy with more important things.

I took an aggressive bite of bread. I had to get back somehow—apologize to Lord Hades if I had to, but I had to go back. The work here left me feeling exhausted and small. Worse than useless. I shouldn't have to live like this.

I missed beauty and cheer and sunshine and my little reading shed. Here, I'd wither. Hades had to understand that...

Remembering his eyes as they caught mine in the garden, I wasn't so sure. He demanded what he wanted and expected all orders to be followed. Every line spoke of power. I felt it even thinking about him.

I was deathless, but nothing compared to Hades.

"Excuse me, Lord Hades, but I need to leave."

"I don't give you my permission."

"But I'm languishing here."

"Then languish. But do the job I brought you here to do."

"What if I can't?"

"Then you deceived me." His voice became smoother as he approached, holding forth his miraculously uninjured hand. The cut of his jacket accentuated the animal grace of his muscles as he drew closer.

I blushed, taking his hand and letting him pull me flush against him. "Lord Hades..."

I blinked, taking another bite of the bread. No. No no no, that wouldn't do. Why was my imagination running that way? Dreaming about characters in a book was one thing, but imagining scenarios with Hades himself was something else. Everybody who met him probably imagined... something. He was too beautiful and powerful to avoid thinking about. And he smelled really, really good. Just because he turned his intoxicating attention to me for a second didn't mean I could let him parade all over my mind. It was indecent. Besides that, he had stolen me away from my home. He wasn't a good person, even if the shadow of scruff on his jaw played tricks with my mind.

How long would he keep me here if I couldn't perform? He appeared to value efficiency. Maybe he would trade me for someone else.

Complicated emotions greeted that thought. I did want to go home, more than anything, but I also wanted to finally succeed in helping these poor humans, not get traded away. Hades had said he'd pay for two more gardeners to take my place. With a snap of his fingers, I could be replaced here too.

I chewed my lower lip. The longer I stayed, the longer I got in the way of people who could actually help.

It was settled. I'd apologize to Hades and request to leave.

Casting my eyes at the door, I cleared my throat. "Marzanna?" I'd never called for her before. It felt a little like summoning a demon.

Or maybe that's exactly what it was.

I played with the crust in my fingers. Did I have to wait for Marzanna at all? I wasn't a child. I could explore the halls myself and discover wherever Hades was. His presence felt so large that I didn't doubt I could find him.

"Marzanna?" I tried again.

Huffing a breath, I angled upright. This was ridiculous. Lord Hades was busy but I'd be quick. Even if I had to wait a few days until he could arrange for me to return, that would be fine. At least I'd have closure. An answer. Something other than the despair of wide, unseeing eyes I was powerless to help.

I slipped on dry shoes and padded to the door, my heart thumping. I wouldn't get in trouble for this, would I?

Marzanna's warning returned to me. Don't go out of your room, she'd said. My hand froze on the door handle. It had been phrased like advice and not an order, hadn't it? My mother's voice thundered through my mind. *Don't do it. Stay put. Stay safe.*

Feeling reckless, I peeked out, pressing one eye to the crack in the door. Nothing but an empty hall. There were no creatures of the night lurking to gobble me up. Goddesses couldn't permanently die, but they could suffer. Mother made me painfully aware by her looks and hints that there were still many things to fear.

I swung the door open wider, looking right and left. A cold

breeze was the only one to greet me. Marzanna's antlers were nowhere in sight.

"I'm sorry, Mother," I said under my breath.

And I went to find Hades.

The castle was huge, desolate, the opposite of Kantharos in every way. In the gardens, we lived in eternal spring. Here it seemed eternal winter. Perfect angles and precision were the only similarities I could find. High overhead, the gray ceiling met the gray walls in a severe line like the slice of a knife.

I marched down the most obvious way. Hades would reserve the most important space for himself, where all the hallways led, I guessed.

What would his private suite look like? (I imagined it had to be a private suite.) Maybe all-black marble. A massive tank set into one wall with a toothy shark inside. Austere furnishings. A circular bed with black sheets and a polished black headboard carved like an ocean wave. The corners would be smudgy with spirits. I pictured him standing there, hands clasped behind his back, the merest hint of a smirk on his face.

"Is something wrong?"

Breathless, I emerged from my reverie. Marzanna had just come around a corner, her fearsome silhouette heightened by a blazing lantern just behind her. I couldn't see her expression. Everything was too dim.

"No," I said quickly. "I just wanted to see Lord Hades." Those answers didn't make sense together. Either I had to see him about an emergency, or I shouldn't be looking for him at all.

Marzanna shifted out of the backlight until I could see the

expression on her black lips. "My lord is not seeing visitors now."

"May I see him in the morning?"

Marzanna glided forward. My stomach flipped with the eerie feeling that she really was a spirit herself. "If you are ill, a doctor will attend to you."

"I'm not sick. I just…" I sighed. Any compassion I hoped to find in her strange gaze was missing. "You've seen me at the wharf. I'm trying my hardest, but I can't seem to help anyone. My power isn't strong enough."

"Lord Hades thinks it is."

"It isn't."

"Try again."

"But—"

"Those are his orders." Her voice shifted into menace.

My throat closed. I blinked at the ground to avoid her flashing eyes. Marzanna was a goddess far more powerful than I was. Everyone here was more powerful. Even Tos at the docks.

"What is the song?" Her question came out a little more gently.

"I know it, but—"

"Sing it."

I stared at her in disbelief. She wanted me to recall the Singers' song in this deserted hallway? It almost felt like a fault against the dead. "Are you sure?"

The antlers bobbed.

I couldn't disobey. She had already found me wandering the castle alone. Worse than that, I admitted I was looking for Hades. He had no time for me and my woes. A chill pierced my body before I carefully began the ghostly tune.

"Wind and bone,

fire and flesh,

answer my call,

the call of the word.

The spirit awaits,

the moon and tide rise.

Gather again

before the glow dies."

Burning replaced the chill on my cheeks as I finished. Marzanna stood as unmoved as a forest creature for several long breaths.

"Good," she finally said. "You know the song. Now save the spirits."

My mouth fell open. "It's not that simple. You know it isn't!"

"I know Lord Hades' orders. You will try to save the humans."

Her tone was the one Mother used when arguing was useless. I clamped my teeth shut. I wouldn't give up, either on my job or on trying to get Hades to let me go. For tonight, I had to add another failure to the pile.

Marzanna's flowing white skirt floated next to my purple one. She knew I liked bright, feminine dresses and brought me a new one every day. Even the heavy, fur-lined gowns were pretty. They were being so generous.

I had to let go of some of my frustration. Since I couldn't ask where Hades was, I mustered the courage to ask a different question. "Would you mind bringing me a couple books to read tonight?"

"Which titles?"

If I couldn't escape bodily, at least I could escape into books. But now I had to admit which books I liked. No one, not even Mother, knew the stories that captured my secret heart. They were harmless fantasies, but I knew she would disapprove. I was good, obedient, and tried to be caring... but I liked a darker kind of romance. That flower shed with its steamy books was my favorite refuge. Both sides of me. So personal that the memory of losing it stung like a new wound.

I flexed my toes in my shoes and steeled myself. "*Dracon Unbound* and *Everlasting Desire*."

I couldn't watch Marzanna's reaction. Maybe she'd judge me. *And I just told her I was looking for Hades.* The combination flooded me with mortification. "If you don't have those, anything's fine," I sputtered.

"I shall get you the titles you requested." Her tone was unreadable.

I chanced a look. Amusement deepened the soft lines around her mouth, but she wasn't quite smiling.

Exhaling, I said, "Thank you."

A piece of home. It was just what I needed. Reading more about Dracon and Esmeralda would give me the strength for another day. Hopefully there wouldn't be many more to endure. Because despite Marzanna's warning, I still had to find a way to reach Hades and get his permission to leave.

We reached my room in only a few steps.

"Lock the door," she ordered.

I bit the inside of my lip in irritation, but did what she said once she left. Locked in a stone castle like some forgotten, frozen fairy tale. But my life was no fairy tale. I had an impossible task that chilled my blood and fogged my brain with hopelessness.

Beneath my fingers, a few more slender flower stems grew around the window. I was running out of space. Could I do the same thing with the walls?

Rebellion hardened within me. First, I'd coat this entire room with flowers, just to prove that I'd been here and that I was trying my best, even if I couldn't do exactly what the god of the dead commanded.

I'd read my books, not caring if Marzanna judged me for them.

And I would track down Hades. Tonight. Surely Marzanna couldn't be everywhere at once. I'd find out when the halls were empty. We had encountered no fearsome creatures like she described. Maybe her stories were just that—stories.

The Far Realm was creepy, savage, but this castle seemed all but abandoned. The more I thought about it, the angrier I became. What right did they have to kidnap me and then hold me captive with ghost stories?

I didn't realize a clump of mushrooms arched out from the corner, growing wildly, branching out in bizarre shapes and angles, until Marzanna appeared. She didn't comment on the new growth, but she gave the corner a pointed look before handing me the volumes I requested.

"Thank you," I murmured.

Her black lips thinned in an unreadable look. I didn't think it was amusement this time.

"It's getting late," I guessed. The storms outside prevented me from ever really knowing.

"Indeed."

She could have been a sphinx for how inscrutable she was.

"I'll be fine the rest of the night, I think." I lifted the books. "I'll try again tomorrow." I weighed my words, unwilling to lie and unwilling to stay put until tomorrow.

"Good. Call if you are in need." With an inclination of her head, she backed out of the room.

I cocked my ear to listen for her steps fading away. I couldn't hear a single one. The silence unnerved me. Would I be able to tell she'd retreated to her own room, if she had one? It was a strange thought. I had a much easier time picturing Hades' private space than Marzanna's.

My own breathing and the wind against the window were the only noises.

"I'll be back," I whispered to the books as I set them down on the blankets. Only then did I notice what they looked like. Before, I'd been too intent on other things. Buttery leather with intricate designs embossed in red and gold formed the covers and spines. I ran my thumb over them, in awe. The copy I'd managed to procure at home was little more than a bound manuscript. All the better for escaping notice.

A tug of guilt pulled behind my sternum. I hadn't meant to defy Mother. I simply liked the books, and they were harmless, right?

With another fond stroke, as though they had become my prized pets, I left the books and tiptoed back to the door. This time I would try going in the opposite direction, methodically searching the castle until I found—

A crash against the door sent me stumbling backward. My skin crawled and ice shot through my veins. What was that?

It sounded heavy. Very heavy. And not as though it had

fallen against the door. This was an attack by something vicious and large. I tried to catch my breath, half-crouched by the bed. My eyes darted to the icy sconces in the walls. Could I pull them off to defend myself?

Another explosion of sound, followed by wrenching claws splintering the wood. Nothing had burst through yet. This thing seemed awfully determined, though. How long could the thick door hold it off? And what *was* it? The beasts and demi-gods I'd already met were enough to terrify everyone in my former life. If Marzanna wanted to warn me about this one, what could it possibly be? I couldn't conjure an image of anything that matched the thumps and snarls and scrapes.

Finally, I remembered. "Marzanna!" I cried, afraid to raise my voice.

A thick crack rent the door diagonally from top to bottom. I bit back a shriek.

"Marzanna," I whispered. "Help!"

What did I think would happen? She'd appear like a ghost?

A heavy claw forced its way through the thin opening. My lungs stopped. It was as long as my middle finger. Terrified tears stung my eyes.

I stood no chance if it breached the door. I still had no idea what it was.

"What the fuck!" The deep voice cried out sharply, too far away.

The door popped, another piece of wood giving way under the monster's attack.

I'm sorry, Mother. I'm sorry, Libera. I'm sorry, Hades.

I shut my eyes tight. How did anyone brace themselves for

something like this? I clenched my muscles, trying not to hold my breath.

I'm sorry.

A shadow passed over my eyelids, then a tearing, and a screech. It sounded like a fight between feral animals fighting over prey. I flinched.

Quiet fell, punctuated by my panicked sniffs.

A faint squeak of hinges. My heart climbed into my throat. It was inside. This was it.

"Persephone, are you all right?"

When I cracked one eye open, it wasn't an unspeakable monster or Marzanna answering my call who stood there.

It was Hades.

❧ II ❧

HADES

I tasted blood on my lips. Lumps of fur and flesh were the only signs the manticore had ever stood there.

I swallowed down bile. This was a creature shunned by its own country, one of only a handful left in the world. In life, it was magnificent, its sleek lion head glowing with animal gratitude when I allowed it to stay. I still hadn't found it a permanent home—one on a long list of things to do. Apparently, I should have moved that up to a priority. If it hadn't been so enraged, and if the door wasn't shattering, I would have spoken to it, forced it to calm down. But I had no time. The manticore's death came too suddenly, too violently.

I plucked out a handkerchief and ran it over my face. Smeared dots of blood soiled the cloth. I glowered at it before tucking it away again.

The manticore had been attacking Persephone. That level of unprovoked aggression would not be tolerated in the Far Realm. My shadow made sure of that.

Had I not fed the manticore enough? Not cared for it?

I shrugged my second self on like another skin, but it was restless now. Two kills in quick succession? I felt it churning inside me, excitable, claws ready to slash. Internally, I snarled for it to behave. Always straining against the leash, that one.

Stepping around the body, I produced a key and opened Persephone's door.

A riot of flowers in the window frame caught me by surprise. I didn't often see that much color at once. Were those mushrooms sticking out of the wall?

Nothing else seemed out of place. The manticore hadn't breached the entrance.

Persephone ducked, half-hidden by the big mattress. Terror distorted her features. Eyes and lips squeezed shut, arms trembling. She looked so small like that. Fragile, even.

So much for the easy conversation I came here for…

"Persephone, are you all right?"

Her eyes popped open and met mine. Shock registered briefly in her look. If that manticore had hurt her somehow, I would hang the corpse of the beast as an example for anyone tempted to do the same thing.

"Yes." She rose, voice hoarse and fists shaking as she clenched the skirt of her purple dress. "What…?"

"Hungry manticore. Possibly bored. You were easy prey."

"Easy…?"

"Yes, but I took care of it."

Her gaze slid past me to the body parts strewn across the marble floor. Her bronze skin went ashy in horror.

"I'll have the door replaced, if you're still comfortable staying here," I went on. "And I'll clean that up."

"I'm not."

"What?"

"I'm not comfortable staying here."

I slid my hands in my pockets. "That's fine. There are plenty of rooms. Just tell Marzanna—"

"No," she said, her voice growing stronger. "I mean, I'm not comfortable in the Far Realm at all, Lord Hades. I tried to do as you asked but I haven't been able to save even one human spirit." Her eyes glossed over with tears, making the beautiful contrast to her skin even more evident. She really seemed to care about the humans. Not too many cared about the dead. Not enough, anyway.

"That's what I came here to talk to you about," I said. "Marzanna told me you were struggling to heal the bodies. I had a moment, so I came to hear your side, ease your worries."

"That's it," she said with a little shrug. All her movements were so simple and graceful, as if she belonged in a different world entirely, one that had easy answers and glowing joys. "I've tried everything I can think of and nothing works. My power isn't strong enough for this."

Annoyance flared. I removed my hands from my pockets to massage one palm. The small mark still hadn't gone away. "You've been here a week. You think that's enough time to test the limits of your power?"

Persephone frowned, chest still rising and falling visibly as she recovered her breath. A fierce little flame lit in her eyes. The creature within me tested the confines of its cage, straining with shameless demands, but I hushed it. My gaze fell before rising again to her face. She didn't seem to notice.

"I think so," she answered. "I've put everything I have into this job."

I smiled humorlessly. "Everything. That's a load of shit."

Her mouth fell open, outraged. "I'm not joking! I'm not trying to trick you to send me home. I've done my best."

I advanced a few steps. Strawberries wafted up to me. Persephone was fresh and earnest, but she didn't know the half of what she could do. I was sure of it. "You healed me on command when you had never even *tried* before. You make flowers from nothing."

"That's—"

"You've always doubted yourself. Mother's not looking over your shoulder anymore. I need you to do this job and I wouldn't have brought you here if I thought you couldn't do it."

Her big blue eyes rounded. Quiet defiance brewed in their depths. I didn't meet with much defiance like this, tentative, learning to stand up for herself. I liked it a little.

"Please don't pretend to know everything about me, Lord Hades. You've met me once—"

"Twice."

"—and I know my own power, my own body." For some inconceivable reason, she blushed deeply. "I know when I'm at my limit," she said more quietly. "And I'm about to reach it. Please let me go home, my lord."

I studied her for a moment. "I formally apologize about the manticore." I clenched my jaw at how brutal *my* attack against it had been. If my shadow self had killed it in a less brutal way, maybe Persephone could have brought it back to life for practice. Wishful thinking. "But you're staying here."

"You won't take me home?"

I eased back on my heels. "I will not."

Her role was too crucial. With as many bodies that were

delivered to the wharf every week, I had to find a new way to offer humans an afterlife. For the people themselves and for their families who had sent them across the Stygian Sea with a prayer and two coins.

I wasn't exactly a kind god, but I cared about second chances.

If Persephone could reunite souls and bodies, it would be revolutionary. I wouldn't give that up now because she struggled with self-esteem issues.

"Here," I said, "grab your things. I'll put you up in a new room for the night until I can get this one cleaned up."

Persephone had gone mute when my response didn't go her way. She was clearly holding in all she wanted to say. Probably taught to be quiet. I almost wished she would continue to fight back. But it was better that she didn't.

The monster inside didn't need another excuse to make me tighten the leash.

I didn't have anything to gather except my books and nightgown. Under Hades' watchful eye, I almost left the books lying on the bed, but couldn't stomach being away from them. Without any other company, I needed them desperately. A little piece of home.

Anger seized my throat as I wrapped the silky gown loosely over the volumes.

"Ready?" Hades cocked a brow, his handsome face set. Nothing I could say would change his mind to let me leave. It was cruel.

My attention shifted to the pile of manticore dead at the entrance to my room, and I fought to swallow. Even a monster attack wasn't enough to convince him to release me. What else roamed these halls? My voice had nearly gone when I answered, "Okay."

Hades strode out, avoiding the creature's body, all its viscera spread across the hall. I felt sick, but I followed. My heart tugged at leaving my flowers. Without me, they'd wilt. Maybe I could return to tend to them tomorrow.

I tripped along, struggling to keep up with Hades' quick, sure pace. He moved like an animal or a lord. *Or a god.* Inwardly, I rolled my eyes at myself. Of course he walked like he owned the place. He did.

Even with the threat of another manticore prowling nearby, it was difficult to look at anything but Hades, and impossible to forget his power. If the god of the dead refused me, there was no one I could turn to for help.

Suddenly, he stepped to the side and indicated I should enter the new room first. His expression betrayed nothing. Maybe he felt nothing about my situation. To him, I was just a tool.

As I passed him, his power seemed to charge between us, strengthening when forced into a smaller space. I felt him more the closer I got, almost as if he pressed against me, although we weren't touching. I held my breath until I got inside the room.

When I entered, my heart beat as if I'd passed a dangerous obstacle and made it through safely. I exhaled.

And blinked in surprise.

This space was even grander than the last one had been, done entirely in velvet black. It was a cozy black, inviting and mysterious—not the black of funerals. This room wanted me to bury myself deep within its folds and forget about the rest of the world. In a way, it felt like the inverse of my reading shed back home. There, all was color and life. But this *felt* similar, somehow.

Instead of a traditional bed, a huge mattress took up one corner of the floor, piled high with pillows. Draperies framed a wide fireplace. Curvature in the stone led around a corner as though another room awaited. And maybe most magical of all, a chandelier of alternating jewels and lights cascaded from the impossibly high ceiling, like a waterfall of stars.

"If you want to return to your old room, I can arrange that in a few days."

I whirled. "This is beautiful! I like both."

Hades' gaze took in my bright purple dress. I suddenly felt self-conscious, standing out like this. For all his brooding darkness, Hades blended in better than I did. Maybe Libera was right about earth tones after all—here, I hadn't seen a single bright, natural color. But I wouldn't tell Marzanna my thoughts when she brought me new clothes. In a moment, Hades would look away and I wouldn't have to worry about my clothes drawing his eye. I could just enjoy wearing a lovely purple dress in a sumptuous room.

Alone.

In the Far Realm.

Where I couldn't perform my one task.

"Very good," Hades said. He broke his attention from me. I could all but hear it snap, relieved and disappointed at the same time. "Marzanna will fetch you in the morning."

I opened my mouth to speak but he was already gone.

Remembering the manticore, I locked the door behind him. This one wasn't made of wood, but polished metal. The room should have felt colder or more ominous, but *it* wasn't the problem. In fact, my stomach squirmed, I liked it so much.

My situation in general was the problem. Hades was the problem—the way he acted like I didn't know myself and refused to let me go. He was a big, intense wall I couldn't walk through. I'd explained myself clearly, hadn't I? And I'd been polite. I didn't want to leave because I was weak or even afraid. It would be better for everyone.

I dumped the nightgown and books on the shadowy mattress, then flung myself down after them. This bed was three times the size of my last one, and I'd thought *that* was magnificent. This one swallowed me like a warm sea. When I kicked off my slippers, black silk curled around my bare feet. It was delicious. I gathered an armful of blankets and breathed in the smell. Like mint and musky rain. Like Hades.

I grabbed *Dracon Unbound* and propped myself up on my elbows to read. No use being angry all night. Soon enough, Marzanna would appear at my door like an apparition to usher me outside in the rain. No chance I'd sneak out of my room again after what just happened. And why would I? I'd spoken to Hades, as I wanted, and I'd gotten nowhere.

Dracon and Esmeralda's story enveloped me like steam. I was home in my reading shed.

"Leave me, Esmeralda," Dracon breathed, his vicious mouth nearly against the skin of her neck. She imagined she could feel the points of his canines already pricking her.

"No." She leaned against him instead, arching backward to give him more access to her blood.

His hot breath warmed her throat. An animal growl ripped from his mouth, and he was on her.

Esmeralda's heart beat wildly as he sank his teeth into her flesh, sucking, his noises wanting, desperate to get closer. She squealed, the strange sensation of him drowning all thought.

He closed his muscular arms around her, pinning her down. She surrendered to him with her entire yearning, aching body.

I reached. No water.

My mouth felt gummy. Inhaling, I sat up on my knees, cautiously fingering my own neck right where Dracon bit Esmeralda. What would it feel like to be so desired that a lover wanted not just to taste but devour? The idea made me weak.

I scratched gently with my fingernail. It felt nice, so I gave myself a sharp pinch.

An idea crashed into me. That was it! Another way I could practice. It was probably nothing, probably useless, just like all the other things I'd tried. But if Hades was forcing me to stay, the least I could do was see if he was right. He wanted me to test the limits of my powers. Okay, I'd try one more time.

Exploring the room and dislodging a pin securing one of the draperies, I tested it against my fingertip. That would do.

A little embarrassed, I returned to the mattress and sat cross-legged next to the book. What harm was there in imagining? Squeezing the pin between my fingers, I closed my eyes.

What if Dracon bit Esmeralda's leg next? I felt less apprehensive about piercing my leg than my neck, where too many important veins and muscles ran through. He would lower his head and murmur praise into the skin of her thigh... I flushed and felt for a good spot. *Then his teeth would go in.* The pin mirrored the movement, a bite hard enough to spread a luscious ache through my limb.

And then my arm. A prick sank into my forearm and I

gasped, growing wet. No telling if this was wrong or innocent. It felt wrong.

And then... My chest was heaving now. *My breast.*

I pictured Dracon's piercing eyes staring up at me as he closed his mouth over the tender skin. I winced as his teeth knifed into me. Maybe he'd suck...

I let my head fall back. My pulse throbbed hard between my legs. I pricked myself again a second time before coming to myself.

My cheeks flamed. What had I just done? This was vulgar. How had I even come up with such a coarse, unseemly idea?

Blinking away the haze of desire that still lingered, I peered down at the exposed skin of my leg. A drop of blood beaded, almost black against the skin.

The sight took me back to Hades in the garden, when he'd cut himself and ordered me to fix him. And I realized I hadn't pictured some faceless, beautiful vampire when I thought of Dracon. This time, I had pictured Hades. It was him murmuring against my skin, his teeth deep into my breast.

My face grew hotter. It felt like my cheeks were expanding. *Wrong, wrong, wrong...*

I set the pin down in a safe place and ran my thumb over the new wound. I hadn't just done this for... pleasure. I'd done it to test myself.

Drawing on my strength, I closed my eyes and felt for the life within. If I could draw out enough, I should be able to heal myself. At least that was approximately the method for healing plants. It wasn't hard to find life. I knew my body and the spirit within intimately. The only difficulty was drawing the life forward. It was like trying to apply pressure to oneself. You couldn't push yourself backward, and I met similar resistance now.

You can do it. Hades was convinced I could, so there had to be a small possibility he was right.

Something rose beneath my fingers, a tingling, a stirring. I followed it with my mind as it circled the small puncture wound.

Finally, the stirring stopped. I opened my eyes. When I moved my thumb, there was no more mark. A grin spread across my face.

I tried again with the forearm injury. That one was easier.

At last, my soft breast with its two cuts. I shoved away the vivid image of Hades looking up at me from where he sucked worshipfully.

I hadn't even pulled my dress down completely. There was no reason my mind should concoct such lewdness. It was wrong in so many ways.

But, in the wake of this small victory, when my mind returned to Hades, I gave myself the reward of letting it linger.

I FOUND THE LEAST MANGLED CORPSE. MY VICTORIES LATELY were so small that I tried to revel in each one—the storm wasn't as fierce today, I didn't feel as cold, I'd managed to heal my tiny wounds from the night before. Hopefully, that practice would pay off here.

The young man had a sword thrust to the chest. It was one injury, simple enough for me to understand and maybe heal.

I frowned as I peered down. His mouth ratcheted open, eyes tightly shut. Under my fingers, the body felt cold. Doubt tore over me like a wave. I'd failed so many times. Why would this be any different?

I pressed the pad of my finger against my forearm, remembering how it felt when the skin and muscle knit together. It was strong and visceral, so much more potent than curing flowers. I could do that almost without thinking. This—healing myself, healing Hades—had taken all my concentration.

Hades believed I could do it, and he was ancient and powerful. He'd seen much more than I had in my short life. Wasn't it possible he was right? I bunched my lips to the side. It didn't feel like it.

Try to have hope.

Exhaling, I unbuttoned the torn uniform of the man to expose his chest. The blade had ripped through just over his heart. A fatal blow. Rain washed off the discolored blood as I prepared to try again.

Brow furrowed, I closed my eyes, feeling for life within. I needed some life to meet my hands for the healing to work. It was my life I'd summoned last night in my new bedroom, and Hades' life that had flowed through me like liquid static, awakening my bones and guiding my fingers. I touched the corpse like a blind woman. If there was the faintest spark of life, I'd find it.

The haunting melody of the Singers floated on the wind. Their vessels were too full to help if this didn't work.

I bit back my distaste and kneaded his unresponsive

muscles. Somewhere, there had to be life. "Come on," I whispered. "I'm here. I'm here to help you. Where are you?"

My pointed finger sank into the wound. Nausea threatened, but I felt around. Still nothing.

Why couldn't I do this? Why did all these humans have to die permanently because of me?

Anger replaced my sadness. This was cruel, all of this. My entire body shook as I opened my eyes again. Gritting my teeth, I placed the last flower crown I'd made onto his dark head and kissed it.

An apology rose to the back of my tongue, but I couldn't say the words.

I couldn't take any more. If Hades wouldn't help me, I'd find some way to help myself. Monsters or no, there had to be a way to get off this island safely. Maybe a sympathetic friend I could make, or I could attempt stepping through the air like I did with Hades to get here.

I had tried my hardest. I attempted to see the good in the situation. But all for nothing. If I remained, Drakaina would find me among the bodies one day. Did goddesses taste different than humans? I shuddered. My consciousness wouldn't die, even if my body was destroyed. I couldn't fathom a more terrible fate.

This wasn't the kind of adventure I dreamed of in the royal gardens. Surprise sparked in my core when the memory of the gardens felt like returning to a different prison.

I was being dramatic. There was nothing confining about those gardens. There, I had people who cared for me. I had a job I could do well. It was beautiful. But my heart couldn't help longing for another option, far away from piled corpses or rigidly aligned shrubbery. Something like Dracon's castle with its temptations and treasures and quests to far-off places.

I sank back on my heels, squirming with guilt—guilt about the indecent desires that pushed in more and more often, guilt about my attitude toward home, guilt about the dead young man in front of me.

I'd leave the terrible Far Realm, that much I knew. But then, where did I really belong?

HADES

"Fuck! You're joking." I squared my jaw, fighting not to fiddle with my hair, my cuffs, anything to release this energy building inside my ribs. I had to remain in control if I had any chance of maintaining order.

I inhaled deeply. Exhaled. Lowered my head.

Marzanna wasn't flustered by my outburst. She'd seen far worse.

"Who the *fuck* does Lox think he is to send all the Mayari here? I'm not here to cater to his megalomania." I pinched the bridge of my nose. "I can't handle this right now. Tell him no. All the extra land I have is some barren space I'm trying to prepare for the human spirits. Unless there is real need, the Far Realm is not accepting any further cases." I opened my eyes to meet Marzanna's. "I assume they're not stirring up trouble in Hyperion? The Mayari have always kept to themselves, I thought."

"As did I."

No, Lox wanted to banish them because he perceived a

threat to his reign. Mayari were powerful demi-goddesses, beautiful, adorers of the moon. I'd only seen one once, and the sight had burned my skin. I understood why humans revered them. But representing the night didn't equal disrespect to the day. If Lox's ego weren't so fragile, he'd understand that. But he had to take his role as god of the sun so literally. All light, all wisdom, all music. Beneath that glow he was sicker than I was. Well, maybe that was an exaggeration.

"We're not accepting the Mayari. They're fine where they are," I repeated. If personal vendettas against entire groups came into play, I'd be overrun. Gods were fickle and jealous. If I allowed it, multitudes would gather on my shores, banished for being indifferent or handsome or intelligent. No reason too small to get rid of someone, as I well knew.

My job was difficult enough with the human dead, Abaddon prisoners, and individual outcasts. My skin felt tight. My patience was running out.

"Shall I fetch you a cup of wine, my lord?"

"No." I still had a full day ahead of me. Once I finished, I would have *several* cups of wine, not just one.

"Very well, my lord."

"Has the body been disposed of in front of Persephone's room?" A twinge of unease shivered through my body at the memory of last night. I wasn't sure why, which bothered me.

"It has."

"And the room prepared for her again?"

Persephone had said she liked both rooms—surprising given her preference for bright, sunny colors. I'd always had a penchant for the darker ones. I almost smiled.

"Yes, my lord."

"Has she recovered any spirits yet?"

"No one has witnessed it."

My eyes slitted. "Is she trying, like she says?"

"My powers lie elsewhere," Marzanna replied. It wasn't an answer.

I grunted in response.

If anything, Persephone did sound sincere. Everything about her was sincere. From her words to her big eyes to her pretty mouth. I was disposed to believe her more readily than most. She believed she couldn't help the dead. But I had felt her power knitting my flesh back together. It wasn't an experience I'd soon forget.

"Anything else?" I asked, clipped.

"Xiope sank two corpse boats that strayed too far north."

A rogue siren. Just what I needed.

Sirens inhabited this kingdom before I even arrived. We had an agreement: no sinking boats without my express permission. Yet another loose end to track down. Xiope would have to be punished, and it wasn't easy to punish a siren. Good thing I was the most frightening creature on this island when I needed to be. But I didn't want to be. I wanted something to go fucking right, for once.

"Any *good* news?" I bit out.

Marzanna's black mouth stretched in a grim facsimile of a smile. Not today, apparently.

I glanced at the map on the wall, mentally ticking off the tasks and locations. "I'll take care of it."

What I wanted was an outlet for my pent-up frustration. Something cathartic involving pain. No permanent damage, only measured chaos. A chance to unleash. Maybe even with willing participants.

I stuffed the thoughts away. They tasted too much like strawberries, and I didn't need something else to worry about.

A claw ran between my ribs, tantalizing, lascivious. *Call her here*, the shadow insisted.

I didn't do sex, and I certainly didn't do it with an innocent thing like Persephone. Seeing her tremble last night... My cock twitched to think of it. I scowled. If it was even remotely a good idea to indulge that particular fantasy, I'd destroy her. I'd worked fucking hard to overcome my monstrous tendencies around my subjects, to give them a ruler they could respect. I wouldn't throw it away because I felt stressed and the idea of stroking Persephone's trembling body turned me on.

Here, I was her king and her protector. She worked for me. That was the full extent of our relationship.

"Do you think the other sirens would agree to help Persephone practice her powers?" I asked suddenly. It was a long shot, but if they met, maybe I could solve two problems at once, at least temporarily. I needed all the breathing room I could muster.

"I will send someone to request their presence, my lord."

"At the plain." Sending them to the barren spot I hoped to use for spirits one day (after it wasn't such a blight) would pull sirens from the coast and Persephone from the sight of corpses, which seemed to bother her so much. Maybe deathless females of destruction could teach a goddess of life something about her innate ability. Unlikely, but it meant a distraction for both parties who needed to be relocated for now.

Good enough.

"Set it up."

❧ 14 ❧

PERSEPHONE

What would Mother think if she could see me now?

I'd heard of sirens. Everyone had. Tales of shipwrecks and maneaters had set my skin tingling in pleasurable terror when I was a girl. They were cautionary illustrations of what would happen if you strayed off the right path.

As I followed my guide—a short, horned being with gray skin and a pleasant face—across the remaining distance of barren rock, I felt like I had definitely strayed off the right path somehow. If I had acted correctly and been good, how did I end up in the Far Realm tending to dead bodies and approaching a siren face to face?

I hugged myself. Surprisingly, when I craned my neck up, I could see blue sky through streaky patches of gray cloud. No rain fell. The temperature would have been pleasant if the deadly chill of fear didn't coat my skin.

Marzanna had provided me with a yellow gown this time, fitted with a fur mantle and draped with a semi-transparent embroidered overlay. I was horribly conspicuous. Here, on the rocks, there was nothing to break up the monotony of hard gray stone but me. If any predators lurked, I'd be their first target.

If.

I *knew* predators lurked. Sirens were experts at luring in their victims, and here I was, walking straight to meet them.

"Hades thinks they might help," Marzanna said before handing me off to my guide.

"They?"

"There are seven."

"I'm meeting all of them at once?"

"It is my lord's wish."

"Aren't there eight sirens, like the eight rulers of the Realms?"

"One is indisposed."

I'd never heard of a siren being indisposed. Maybe eating sailors made for stomachaches.

Thin black figures appeared on the horizon, like flower stems. My breath shortened.

Had Marzanna lied? Was I being punished for failing? How could deadly sirens possibly help my situation?

A full day of trying to figure out how to escape the Far Realm had yielded no ideas. The night drew me back to Dracon and Esmeralda, whose encounters left me breathless and mercifully distracted. In the morning, I'd woken up to news of my meeting with the fabled sirens. If they held the key to escaping this place, I didn't see it.

The figures grew larger as we approached. The sirens varied in everything but beauty and horror. Each distinct being was designed to lure people in with her exquisite beauty, but, in the barest shifts of cloud light, glimpses of the monster flashed beneath. Luxurious skin with silken scales and fangs.

My heart thumped painfully. I turned to my guide. "You're staying, right?"

"I'm afraid I have other duties."

My face went cold. "When will you... pick me up?"

"You saw the way."

Directions had been pretty simple. We traveled through the air a certain distance to the west, then walked in a straight line over the rocks to meet the sirens. I could probably find my way back on my own. Despite all that, I didn't want to be left alone with these alluring, terrifying creatures. Was everything in the Far Realm designed like this? Hopelessly tempting but monstrous just underneath?

"You won't come back for me?" I tried again. With any luck, I didn't sound as desperate as I felt. The eyes of the fearsome sirens burned my neck as I turned away from them.

The gray-skinned creature blinked slowly, unconcerned. "You saw the way."

His repetition grated. "Okay."

"Go with the Divine." It was an old greeting, even by deathless standards, but I echoed it.

Without another word, the guide left me alone with seven deadly sirens.

Mouth dry, I turned.

"This is Hades' girl?" one with dark skin hissed, but it sounded almost like a purr. A whisper to make me come closer, to pull me down...

"I'm not Hades' girl," I said, already flustered.

A different siren pulled up short at my answer, excitement

mingling with her annoyance. She cast a glance at the one who had spoken first. *Prey*, it said.

My heart felt like a caged animal. "But he's the one who sent me to meet with you."

The excited siren exhaled, obviously disappointed. Her slim greenish arms crossed over her torso, mirroring my posture. She moved gracefully, as though she were underwater.

"Meet with us?" she echoed through a glimpse of razor teeth.

The frightening parts of the sirens made me curious to see more. Did they have spikes, forked tongues, poisoned scales?

"He thought you could... help." Had Hades not told the sirens what they were supposed to do? Did they have similar powers to mine, but chose not to use them? The idea was ludicrous.

The nearest female smiled. All of them, I realized, had slits for pupils. "Help with what?"

In the presence of these fearsome creatures, I felt small and ignorant. This was a silly idea. I looked behind me. Maybe I could just go back.

A hand touched my arm and I stifled the urge to scream. The velvet-soft touch chilled my skin.

When I turned back, they all stared at me as if they could read my mind. Maybe they could. That ability was rare, but not unheard of. I had the odd sensation that they were one many-headed entity sizing up when to devour me.

"I need help bringing the dead back to life!" I blurted.

The dark-skinned siren laughed. "The dead do not live."

"I need to unite their spirits and bodies. Lord Hades brought me here to help him, and I can't do what he wants."

Seven pairs of slitted pupils raked up and down my small form. I could look a couple of these sirens in the face, but they were so much more magnificent, with unearthly violence simmering beneath the surface, that I felt tiny.

"Lord Hades chose you for this task?"

"Yes," I said miserably, eyes falling to the rock at my feet.

"Lord Hades is no fool!"

Someone plucked at my arm, raising it before letting it fall. As one, the sirens began to circle me, scrutinizing. My abs tensed. Would they attack now?

"What ability do you have, girl?"

"My name is Seph. I heal flowers."

"Few flowers on the coast. Can you heal all?"

"I can heal insects. And I fixed a cut on Lord Hades' hand."

Glances met meaningfully around me. "You heal bodies?"

"Small injuries, sometimes."

"We destroy bodies."

I shivered. Their voices rose and fell around me like waves. It was hypnotic. Had I ever heard stories about resisting a siren's song? They weren't singing, exactly, but their voices were musical.

"Sailors come too close," one said.

"They long for our bodies."

"And we long for theirs."

My breathing quickened. They weren't kidding. Lust for violence burned in their eyes.

"I can... show you," I said, cutting through the quieting reverie about murdering sailors.

"Show us?"

"Yes, I can make a flower grow."

The moving figures slowed. "Here?"

I swallowed. *Probably*. "Yes."

"You said you can heal flowers. You create?"

"Something has to be there already, but I can make it grow."

The sirens stepped back.

I inhaled deeply. The air smelled like vanilla and salt water. Crouching down, I placed my palm on the seam between two large stones. Instantly, I felt life within. Maybe all that practice at the dock had honed my skills a little. Normally, in such a barren place, I'd have to search more. Now, I was in tune with even a whisp of life. Coaxing the ground with my fingertips, I made a pink bloom rise out of the crack.

When I straightened, a new expression dominated the seductive sirens' faces. I couldn't put my finger on it. Wariness?

The greenish one stepped forward, slowly as before, but with purpose. She pointed to the ground. "You draw life from dead things?"

I shrugged. That wasn't quite right, but she obviously had more to say.

"Why do you glance down?" she demanded.

"Wha—?"

"Why do you shrink before us?"

What was she getting at? "I... because you're *sirens*. The terror of the waters."

Matching, toothy grins. Strangely, the fangs didn't make them less alluring. If anything, they enhanced the sirens' beauty.

"Young goddess, you have not begun to use your power. Flowers and insects?"

I had no time to protest how much I liked those things before they went on.

"Lord Hades was right to send you to us. We will teach you so much more."

Then their song erupted from seven throats. I tried clinging to life, but drowned in beauty and pain.

15

PERSEPHONE

Monsters loomed above me, glaring with hungry, glowing eyes.

No... They were breathtaking sea goddesses. Just to be in their presence mesmerized me. Every movement and sound was like the dance of an elegant swimming creature, seductive, dreamlike.

Squinting, I sat up. My hands met something soft. Wasn't I lying on rocks? Nothing felt real.

"You barely fought back," said the greenish siren, observing the back of one perfectly clawed hand.

"Gave in like the men."

"No," one argued. "Not like the men." She swept her arm toward me, but I didn't know what point she was trying to make. That I was female?

"No," someone agreed. "That was something, at least."

I rubbed my head. "What was?" All the watery haziness started to wash my vision clear.

"Our role is death," a siren chanted.

"And yours is life," another echoed.

"Divine balance protects you."

I frowned. They weren't saying I was invincible, right? That was ridiculous. All goddesses were deathless, but they could be hurt, even put into a death-like state if they committed acts terrible enough. Nothing was making sense.

My fist closed as I steadied myself. Soft. Cool.

Floral.

My gaze darted down. A green patch thick with white daisies cushioned my fall, spreading to my outstretched hand.

I'd never grown so much so quickly before. Pride lanced through me like I'd felt after healing Hades' wound. I'd grown all this in seconds, and I had witnesses. All my recent failure welled to the back of my eyes. This, at least, I could still do—I could still draw beauty from a dead land.

The growth contrasted against the rest of the barren landscape. Now this patch of flowers, the terrifyingly beautiful sirens, and my yellow dress stood out against the gray.

"How...?" I began, unsure of how to ask the question.

"You hold the power of spring, of rebirth, of plants that grow and life that's mended." The dark-skinned siren's words soothed me.

"I know, but I've never done that before." I trundled awkwardly to my feet.

"You are not a doer of tricks, but a goddess of life." She looked around at her sisters. "We know who we are. Do you know who you are, young one?"

Not every detail, obviously. I flexed my hands open and closed, trying to feel what it must have been like to pull all this springy growth from little more than stones. Why did I have to be unconscious when it happened?

"Do it again."

The siren's command paralyzed me. I'd heard that order more times than I could count, both from others and myself, at the dock.

Again.

But I can't.

Again.

He's too injured, I—

Again.

I let the spirit get away and now she won't have a second life.

Again.

Please please please come back to me...

My arms shook.

"Again," said the siren.

Tears bit at my eyes. Her command rubbed at all my raw places. "I'll try."

I took a couple steps away from the patch of daisies and bent to the ground. With a furtive look at the intimidating group, I spread my hands over the spot. A little life, but not much. If I had to guess, three small flowers' worth. They bloomed between my knuckles.

"What is that?" snapped a siren with iridescent scales on her neck.

"Flowers."

"Children could do that."

I glared back, suddenly tired of all this. "It's what I can do. I'm sorry if it's not enough for you or for Hades. I'm doing my best."

"Not your best."

"Yes!" I cried. "This is my best."

The greenish siren stepped forward, trampling on my new flowers. I winced when she touched me. "Death is in everything," she said.

Hardly something to make me feel better.

"So is life." She didn't sound as happy about that fact, but she locked eyes with me when she said it. "The world itself is alive. Make it grow."

I hadn't thought of it like that. I thought of my power as searching for seeds and speeding up the usual way of things. With Hades, I'd had the same idea. He was a god. His hand would heal. I would quicken the process.

My eyes found the spongey patch of greenery where I'd fallen. It wasn't an illusion. I'd actually done that.

Maybe the siren was right.

I touched the rock at my feet. One large pink bloom waited to unfurl. I closed my eyes, digging deeper into the ground, into myself, into the trees in the distance, into the sea on the coast, into the depths of soil forming the Far Realm and plunging into the center of the planet. The churning mass of life stole my breath. My other hand joined the first. I was thirsty for more. But how much could I take in?

The land became like my own body. I felt my heart beat deep underground. I breathed in sea water and exhaled clouds.

I ran my hand over the rock, but it wasn't rock. It was thick grass that extended as far as my arm and past my fingertips.

I was drunk. I was powerful.

I was Persephone, the goddess of spring.

Trembling, I opened my eyes. When had I stood up?

Blinking to bring myself back to reality, I saw what I had done. Half of the rocky expanse was covered in lush grass. With a few rogue wildflowers.

The sirens looked back at me with approval as I caught my breath. A grin spread over my face. Never, never, had I suspected I could do something like that. Something so wild and beautiful and powerful.

I knew I was a goddess my whole life, but I hadn't felt like one until now.

I practiced with the sirens until exhaustion overtook me. They were no less terrifying than they were at the beginning, but I learned their names, and now I felt a little dangerous too.

They said goodbye and moved as one toward the edge of the clearing. Back to the ocean, I guessed. To kill more people. I shivered. I had been growing to like them. No one had given me such clear advice before to unlock my power. I owed them. Would they like eating some of the more injured bodies that came to the docks—?

The monstrousness of the idea made my queasy. I hadn't been in the Far Realm long and I was already thinking like this. Mother would have been appalled. I'd think of another way to pay them back for their kindness.

I spun, looking back over the plain. Grass, flowers, and trees grew in swaths over what had been bare rock only hours before. I bit my lip with pleasure. Even though this place had hardened me in some ways, it made me better in others. I was almost grateful that Hades had stolen me away from my regulated life. Back in my bedroom at the castle, I'd keep accessing the power the sirens showed me. I could make the space like my reading shed back home—bursting with greenery and life.

My happy smirk tilted downward. Everything looked different than it had when I arrived. Which direction was home?

I glanced at the sky. No help there. As usual, clouds as dark as night blanketed everything like a low canopy. Even that brief glimpse of blue was gone. Was there any sunshine in the Far Realm? Well, none peeked through the darkness here, so it didn't help with my sense of direction.

The tree line? I'd changed it so drastically that I wasn't sure where I'd come from. Probably over there...? I'd try it, travel in a straight line for a while until (hopefully) I hit the castle. Yes, that looked right.

I stepped through the air, eating up the distance to the trees. Space bent around me. With short distances like this, darkness didn't squeeze my ribs and steal my breath. It was nothing like my journey with Hades had been. This was easy.

My stomach hollowed at the thought of what other creatures lurked in these woods. I'd already met sirens and a manticore. I hurried my pace. The deathless could travel this way, but most supernatural creatures couldn't. I could run away if anything attacked me.

Even if I did make a clear target in my yellow dress.

Faster and faster. Shouldn't the castle be here by now? I'd go a little farther.

There! A dark wall peeked through the trees. I exhaled in relief, making the final jump to it.

But it wasn't the castle. My relief eked away. This wall was enormous, made of ancient stone reaching nearly to the low-hanging clouds. A metal door four times my height was set into the wall with no visible hinges. Cracks spidered out from it as if the door had been smashed into the structure with a massive hand. I glanced upward. What kind of god or creature could do that? A shiver skittered over my bare arms.

Beyond the imposing exterior, the place just *felt* wrong. Almost like vapors from within had leaked out and poisoned the air I breathed. I should have left, but my legs wouldn't move. Fascination and repulsion rooted me to the spot.

What was this place?

I extended my hand, palm outward, to touch the stone. The desire to heal this place, make it beautiful, discover its secrets —*something*—dominated me. Power still pulsed lightly beneath the surface of my skin, the result of the sirens' lesson. In the shadow of this giant place, though, I was shrinking, shrinking, shrinking into myself. Tiny. Conspicuous. In danger.

My palm hit the rough stone. Horror seeped through me like black blood. Evil voices whispered about decay and the end of time. I strained to listen, but the longer I stood there, the weaker I felt, as though my bones were crumbling.

This wasn't right. *I shouldn't be here.*

Something moved to my left. My gut clenched. Darker than the clouds or the wall, it darted like a living shadow. I drew my hand back. Had I awakened something bad? What had I done?

I brought my fists together over my chest as if that could ward off whatever I'd seen.

I hadn't imagined it. The dark figure was tall, savage somehow, but god-like in shape. Even with its hazy edges, the being suggested violence, muscles hard as blades, power beyond reckoning. Maybe this endless wall with its heavy, unopenable door was an attempt to keep this thing contained.

I was no match for it. No one was a match for it.

This being was death incarnate.

My mouth trembled. It was too late. I'd never see my mother or the gardens again. I'd never see Hades. I'd never read another book or take another walk. I'd never give a second life to lifeless humans.

I shrieked as it sprang.

16

HADES

I drew two fingers over my forehead before inhaling the scent of the dark brown liquor in my glass. Spicy and sharp. Hopefully strong enough to distract me for a while. Or at least allow me to sleep.

When my eyes opened, they automatically fell to the spot on the floor where the complete model of the realm lay in my office. My mind couldn't ease its grip on my problems, even when I wanted to relax. There, in my mind's eye, was the large series of barren plains where human souls might be able to find a second life. Not much of a life scrabbling on rocks, though. For now, it was my best bet. The War Twins insisted on sending me more bodies than I could handle. More than I could save...

Xiope the siren obviously had no remorse about sinking the corpse boats, even after I'd calmly explained she had no right to them.

Marzanna assured me she had sent a message to Lox about

not accepting moon goddesses into the Far Realm. Self-absorbed prick. Hopefully, he'd let them live in peace.

I took a long drag of the drink. It burned my tongue and throat, coating them in sweet pain. Another.

I'm not in my office. I need to rest so I can think.

The thought felt like a lie. But it was true. In my effort to somehow disconnect from my responsibilities, my job, my identity, my *self*, I'd sunk onto a settee in my personal suite. Surely a new location would jar me out of the shitshow that was my life recently. Maybe I could even get some sleep. My gaze landed on the large open archway leading to the bedroom. Unlikely.

I took another drink, flicking open the first button at my collar.

"My lord Hades," came an urgent male voice outside the mahogany door.

I rolled my eyes and sat up, biting back a curse.

"Emergency at Abaddon."

My eyes flew wide. I plunked the glass down as I stood, rebuttoning my collar. My shadow self strained like a heavy dog on a leash, making my movements uneven. "Go," I told it.

Darkness peeled out of me, leaving me hollow, as the shadow raced to the prison. He (it didn't like being thought of as an *it*) was better at necessary brutality than I was, and I was pretty good.

I stalked to the next room and ripped open the door. "What kind of emergency?"

The hulking figure swallowed before answering. Half the time, this demi-god guarded the prison doors. In reality, he was only there to convey messages. Only *I* had any chance of keeping the creatures inside contained. Even my blowhard brother Thenios couldn't manage that with all his flashy lightning. He'd never have the balls to take on this responsibility, anyway.

"A newcomer touched the walls."

My mind whirred. Touched the walls, touched the walls... Were they trying to figure out a way to engineer an escape? Who would do that?

Guards were useless against the beings within, so I often had them doing other tasks or patrolling around the circumference of the structure to keep this very thing from happening. "Give me a name."

"I'm not—"

"A name! Who was it?"

The guard's pupils grew small. I needed a name, a description, *something*, and he just stood there like an idiot? I ground my teeth, feeling oddly alone without the constant presence of my shadow.

"She looked young," he finally said.

My skin, already blown cold by this horrible announcement, chilled further. "She. Deathless?"

"She was wearing a yellow dress. Small. Like you."

By that last part, I knew he meant she was like me in basic physique—soft skin, arms, legs, humanoid, like all the Rulers— but my lip curled.

The guard stuttered, realizing his mistake. "Not, that's not —I didn't mean that. Any of that. You're not small." His eyes darted downward, then back up to my face. "Not at all. Not that I would know. You're tall! And she's small, much shorter than you, my lord. The person who touched the wall."

My gods. I'd never seen a bulky guard so flustered. I'd thought he'd be monosyllabic. So much for stereotyping.

Yellow dress, short for a goddess... That sounded like Persephone. But why in the name of the Divine would she have wandered that far from where she was supposed to be?

"Were sirens with her?" I demanded. They were creatures of destruction, after all. Immediately, I doubted my own question. Even the sirens wouldn't dare approach the god-prison unprovoked.

"No, my lord."

"Go." I didn't bother waving my hand. My thoughts whirled chaotically. Anger and confusion colored them all.

Again, I pictured my maps and models. Abaddon was in almost exactly the opposite direction from where Persephone needed to go if she wanted to return to her room. Either of her rooms.

Why was she always getting in trouble? It was bleak enough to picture her scrambling over piles of human corpses, but this?

No one approached Abaddon except the most hellish beings in creation for whom it was made—gods so evil, they had to be contained. I constantly had to commission more wards, more repairs, so they had no possibility of escape. The very idea sent glass shards through my veins.

My shadow appeared in front of me, casting down something bright and yellow. My muscles tightened at the sight of Persephone at my feet. No blood that I could see. My other self hadn't hurt her too badly. If he had, I'd have felt the ghost of his actions on my own skin. Still, he'd carried her here and it wouldn't take much force to damage her—scrapes, lacerations...

My dark alter ego buzzed with rage and lust and violence, openly leering at Persephone's form on the floor. He wanted to be free to punish her, but giving him freedom wasn't an option.

I glared at him, reining him back in with effort. Everything he did was an echo of my own darkest impulses, but I was the restrained one, the one who tried to be reasonable. Even I was finding that difficult now.

Keeping my attention from Persephone was difficult enough to make my fists clench, but finally the shadow self merged back into me.

Damn it if her quiet panting didn't make me think of other reasons she might pant even harder. I knew the phantom sensation of holding her, because my shadow self had held her when he'd brought her here. The claws within me were restless.

She's tasty and wicked, the shadow hissed.

No. Not now. Not ever.

But as I looked down, I couldn't quell the chaos she evoked in me. Delicious, alarming chaos.

17

PERSEPHONE

Blood sparkled in my mouth as the creature flung me down. I caught myself on my hands and knees, but the jolt still jarred through my bones. I stared down at a midnight blue carpet. When had the shadow taken me inside? Probably during one of our jumps through the air. Whatever the violent creature was, it had deathless blood if it could travel like that.

I panted at the ground, trying to gather myself. The rough hands around my waist were gone. The evil-feeling walls were gone. But a sense of dread still clung to me. Where was the shadow being now? He had looked so feral, yet a little familiar too...

Boots appeared in front of me. I looked up. Lord Hades loomed above me, as lordly and magnificent as the room around him. The ceiling stretched so high it made me dizzy from this angle. Glittering blue and black stone polished to a shine. A second story peeked over Hades' shoulder, revealing a glimpse of the sky.

"You're safe," came Hades' voice. His inflection offered no clue what he was thinking. If he was comforting me, it was the comfort a building could offer from a hurricane. The building didn't care if you were in it.

"What?" I gasped, still catching my breath.

The only thing that could have torn my eyes away from those stars in that moment was Hades himself. He wore no jacket, so, even though he still looked immaculately elegant, this was the most casual I'd seen him. A glass with dark liquor dangled from one hand as he looked down at me.

He offered his other hand to me, though his eyes looked dark with a storm of negative emotions. I couldn't tell if that anger was directed at the dark thing that had left me here or at something I'd done. Cautiously, I took his hand, glancing around to find the violent shadow. It had disappeared. Hades hauled me easily to my feet.

I exhaled. Uncertain relief seeped into me through the warm skin of his palm. Even that shadowy thing at the wall was no match for Lord Hades. The gods themselves feared him. And he'd helped me up.

The fabric of his sleeve bunched around his bicep and shoulder as he took a sip from his glass, not taking his eyes off me.

"Now," he said, his voice a low rumble, "why the *fuck* were you at Abaddon?"

I frowned. "The prison?"

Abaddon was the epitome of prisons. Mother told me stories about it to make me behave as a child. Even grown gods and goddesses shuddered at the name. I knew it lay somewhere in the Far Realm, but had I really bumped into *Abaddon* on accident?

"Don't play innocent."

"I'm not! Is that... Was that really the god-prison?"

"Yes, the deathless prison. The god-prison. Home of the most evil entities ever to exist. What were you doing there?" He clinked his glass on a side table beside a reclining couch. Was this Hades' private space?

The question, on top of his piercing attention and the magnitude of trouble I was in for approaching that wall, made my whole body heat. "I didn't mean to," I said. "I didn't know that's what it was. I was just trying to get back—"

"Abaddon is in the wrong direction."

"I didn't know that. I got turned around."

Hades linked his hands behind his back. "How is that possible?"

Apparently, Hades had never been in a new kingdom without anyone to give directions. Or he simply had perfect intuition about where to go. My sense of safety around him was crumbling. Not that I felt in danger, exactly, but I felt *accused.* And I was tired of it. "I didn't know," I repeated, more slowly this time.

"Did you know that the deathless prison houses the most dangerous immortals in history? That if only one escaped, the damage could be catastrophic?"

"I didn't try to free anyone. I didn't even know where I was."

"Inexcusable mistake," he spat, lip curling.

"Then send me back!" I hadn't meant to yell, but I refused to feel bad about it. An hour ago, I'd been a goddess pulling a symphony of life from bare ground. I didn't want to feel like a child again. If Hades didn't think I was good enough, then he could stop berating me and send me back to my old life.

Where I was managed and treated like a child...

Did I really want that?

Hades' eyes flared wide at my outburst. His gaze traced over me as if looking for the source of my defiance. I fought not to squirm under his scrutiny.

"No," he said.

I pursed my lips. No matter where I went, more powerful people controlled me. Would that ever stop?

"Did you meet with the sirens?" he went on. "Could they not help you?"

"They did, actually," I said, standing a little straighter at the memory. My ribs immediately protested. That shadow—where had it gone?—squeezed me tightly enough to bruise. "They were very helpful."

"Except with directions, evidently." He cocked a brow. I sensed annoyance but no more anger. He believed me when I said I meant no harm by approaching the prison. It was a small comfort. Nice to know I had some credibility in his eyes, though.

"I'm still not sure if I'll be able to catch the souls, but—"

"Don't do that."

I opened my hands in irritation. "Don't do what?"

"Constantly second-guess yourself. You'll land in a spiral of self-pity and that helps no one. You made progress. What is it? Explain what you mean." He gestured at the chaise lounge nearby.

I sat, smoothing my dress over my knees.

He scooped up a glass of dark liquid that sat on the end table, apparently ready to listen.

"They... helped me grow grass. There's this rocky area."

"I'm aware of it."

"And they helped me find life under the ground. It was more than I'd ever done before." I turned my eyes up to his. Would he understand how monumental this breakthrough was for me? My lower stomach did a dizzy flip as he met my gaze.

"Grass? That's it?"

I huffed a small, annoyed breath through my nose. Evidently, he didn't care. "And trees, and flowers," I clarified.

"Not exactly a spirit." He took a sip from the rim of the glass.

I frowned. "I didn't have any to practice on. I thought it was pretty impressive."

"Healing me was relatively impressive," he returned, holding up his palm. "Grass is underwhelming."

I stood, rising only to his neck, but at this point, I didn't care. "You weren't there."

"That's true," he conceded, something almost like a smirk lighting his face before the look faded. "But I don't recommend telling me what should or should not impress me," he continued icily. "Facts are far more relevant. Like the fact that you approached the prison."

"Accidentally."

"Did you touch the wall by accident too?"

"No."

"Don't fucking go near there again, Persephone. If you can't tell from my tone, I'm being deadly serious."

I frowned. "I won't."

Clearing my throat, I stepped to the side, giving myself space to breathe. Hades' sharp, direct manner jarred me. Every time I encountered him, he loomed so much larger than me in every sense. Even the way he stood as he questioned me—straight-backed and strong without seeming stiff—spoke of power. His jawline with its dark stubble. His calloused hands. His horrible habit of cutting me off when I spoke.

"Getting as close as you did could have hurt you."

"I heard you," I snapped.

"*Are* you hurt?"

I drew one arm over my waist. The bruises protested. His gaze dropped from mine and more air seemed to fill the room. "No," I answered.

"Did he hurt you?"

The shadow. "Not really. Does the shadow that I saw... Does it work for you? Is it one of yours?" It hadn't reappeared, but the possibility tugged uncomfortably at the back of my mind.

"You could say that," he answered.

I shuddered.

"You said, 'Not really.' Did it?"

"It just held me really hard." I bit my lip. "Just trying to get me away from the wall, I guess." What a stupid mistake. How could I not have sensed the amount of evil coming from that prison?

A low growl emanated from his chest, almost too quiet to hear. "Where?" he demanded. "Where did he touch you?"

Did he think...? "No!" I cried. "He didn't touch me like that. He just... took me away from there." I uncrossed my arms. "My ribs are a little sore. They'll be fine in the morning."

"I would advise that you tell him to fuck off next time you see him, but he doesn't take kindly to criticism."

Next time?

Hades ran a hand through his hair. "Show me where." I could swear his tone softened around the edges—the hint of a purr. He couldn't have meant the question to sound so seductive. My mind was playing tricks on me.

"There," I said dismissively, gesturing in the general direction of my ribs. I didn't like how every meeting with Hades turned into an interrogation.

"I'll deal with him for you."

My eyes snapped back up to his. "You don't have to—"

"Nobody hurts you."

"I was near the prison. It's fine."

He narrowed his eyes. "I know this is hard to believe, but I want my employees to be safe. Even happy, if that's possible."

Employee. The word slammed the professional barrier between us again. I hadn't realized it had started to come down. For a second, I had imagined him lifting off my dress to examine the bruises, vowing vengeance on my behalf, and kissing down my body. Retroactive embarrassment turned my cheeks hot.

Employee. Why did that word hurt more than the bruises?

He sighed, releasing some of his rigid stance. "You have some power," he said. "Could you not feel that going near the prison was a mistake?"

"Not until I touched it." A slight tremor shook me at the memory.

He leaned on the arm of the settee, observing the liquid as it swirled in his glass. "Don't ever do that again." His tone, which had been angry before, now sounded almost... regretful. Like he was looking out for me.

"I know that now," I said. Now that he was leaning, I was a little closer to being able to look at him head on. His deep-set eyes had the faintly bruised look of someone who wasn't sleeping. "I'm sorry."

"Stop apologizing." He downed another swallow, waved his hand. "You made grass grow, you said? How much?"

"It covered about half the plain. That's how I got turned around. The landscape didn't look the same when I left."

"The sirens didn't point you in the wrong direction?"

"No, they were helpful."

"They eat people."

"They can be terrifying and helpful," I challenged, feeling bolder as I thought of the sirens and their power. "Isn't that why you had us meet?"

A smile ghosted the corner of his mouth. "It was." He set down his glass.

"I'm glad they helped you. Will you be ready to try again tomorrow?"

Again, again, again. But this time, I'd had a victory. I still wasn't sure that I'd be able to carry out Hades' command, but *maybe*, this time, I could do it.

I nodded. "Yes."

He regarded me, an odd look in his eyes. "Good."

My heartbeat ran faster the longer he watched me, leaning at his ease like some lounging cat. His presence did things to me I didn't want him knowing about. The embarrassment would kill me.

I forced myself to look past him to the rest of the space.

Twin obsidian pillars flanked an enormous opening leading to another room. That might have been a bed through there. Spiral stairs burst out from both pillars like thorns—one to reach multi-story bookshelves and the other to climb to a tall, windowed chamber. "What room is this?"

"My suite," he answered, his voice rough.

His suite. His private suite, where we were alone.

"I'll take you back to the fortress."

My gaze snapped back to his as he walked past me toward the door. "This place isn't in the fortress? I thought..."

He paused, smiled. "You thought I lived there? God of the dead, ruler of the Far Realm?" He chuckled. "No."

"Then where are we?"

"My palace, but there's no time for a tour."

I gazed up again to the second-story room. Through the ceiling windows, the sky looked clear. No clouds. No storms. Stars. There were stars. Was that an illusion, or were those real? "Are those—?" I cut myself off, afraid my voice would break.

Hades pivoted to follow my eyeline. "What?"

"Stars?" My voice went thick with emotion.

He didn't answer right away, just stood looking at them with me. A thick, silent kind of weight landed between us, like companionship during a momentous event, keeping us in place. "Yes," he finally answered. "The Far Realm is much bigger than the coast."

"I'm sorry. I just haven't seen them since I got here."

"You should be sorry for touching the prison," he said, "not about wanting to see more than storms. Come with me."

I stiffened, unsure. Follow him? Just the two of us together?

It felt dangerous, but then he always felt dangerous to be around. Not in a bad way, usually, but in a strong, overwhelming way.

He didn't look back as he strode to the spiral staircase. I followed, being extra careful since there was no railing.

We ascended until we reached the opening, polished floors stretching to a balcony with a faintly reflecting pool. The ceiling curved above us, scored with windows. In fact, most of it was transparent, giving an excellent view of the night sky.

"My observatory," he said, sweeping one arm out before sliding both hands in his pockets. "The kingdom has fair weather some of the time. The Far Realm is larger than most people realize." The comfortable way he spoke made me proud to be the one to hear it. This felt like a confidence, a glimpse behind the icy façade he showed most people. I had no idea why he was saying these things to me, except that maybe he figured I didn't matter enough to be a threat to his kingdom's secrecy.

"Don't you have other people that can help you, then?" I asked. "Why do you need me?"

"Yours is a rare talent."

The corner of my lips twisted awkwardly with the praise, and my face heated. What was happening? If this moment were in a book, I'd expect more to happen between us, but that was absolutely ridiculous. Fantasy. But my roiling stomach wouldn't listen to reason.

"You said the sirens helped you harness your power," he continued, his voice low. "Show me."

The command sounded indecent when he said it in his rich, cultured way. I had to shake off this feeling. Hades kidnapped me and held me here even though my power failed and my heart broke for those humans. He was far too important and powerful and wicked to notice me that way.

"Are you sure?" I asked. "I don't want to ruin your floor."

He huffed out a frustrated breath. "Persephone, why is it everlastingly about what you *can't* do?"

"Seph," I corrected.

"I prefer Persephone, and I prefer when my subjects trust me."

"Or obey you."

"Yes," he conceded. "I prefer when they obey me."

I sighed, hopefully not enough that he would notice.

Maybe my power wouldn't raise the dead, but I'd remembered something today I wasn't ready to give up.

I *was* a goddess.

I jutted my chin and knelt down. My skin warmed with the acute knowledge of being watched, but I didn't meet Hades' eyes anymore. Before I could doubt myself, I shut my eyes and splayed my hand over the midnight blue marble. Through it, beneath it, there was life. Tiny particles. Enormous root systems. I focused on those, not on the warm, minty smell of the god standing above me.

Inhaling, I called on that life. The floor under my palm grew feathery with grass and flowers. I didn't stop. I was tired of everyone talking down to me, acting like I wasn't trying hard enough.

In the garden, my influence didn't disappear as smoothly as it should.

At home, I didn't stay as young as Mother wanted.

Here, I couldn't obey Hades quickly enough.

I was done.

The plants spread. I couldn't tell how far, but I kept calling to them, caressing their threads of life, healing what was broken. The air around me tanged with magic.

Finally, I sighed and stood. Self-consciousness fought to click into place as it always did. My battle against that feeling was only partially successful.

An evaluating smirk threatened to spread over Hades' face as he observed my handiwork. Now his black and blue quarters had a lumpy carpet of green grass.

Lord Hades was impressed. I had impressed him. Me.

I wasn't prepared for the rush that filled my body. The pride I felt after healing his hand felt small compared to this. He wasn't angry that I'd destroyed his floor. Instead, his eyes practically glowed as they traced the grassy edges all the way to the massive pillars.

Hades rotated back to me. My heart ricocheted against my bruised ribs.

"That," I said. "I can do that."

❦ 18 ❦

HADES

A soft coating of dirt colored Persephone's knees when she stood, the thick scent of a meadow rising around her. Starlight traced the edges of her face.

There was so much life there, so much earnest emotion and love for beautiful things. I wanted to touch her and sop up some of that light to keep for times when darkness threatened to smother me.

But that wasn't how it would go. Still, my chest ached to reach out. What was wrong with me?

"The sirens were good tutors," I mused, toeing the nearest grassy hillock.

Plants grew impossibly on the marble, life bursting through where it had no logical opportunity. The uneven swath of grass reached my feet.

Had her gift stopped after encountering me? I wouldn't have been surprised. She was life. I was death.

But I liked this. I liked this very much.

"You act as if I don't want to save the humans," she said, brows furrowed with intensity. "I do. More than anything, I do. And I'll try again. I don't want you thinking I don't care."

I brushed a dust mote off my sleeve. "You keep asking to return home."

She pursed her lips. "Because I didn't think I could help."

"And now?"

"Maybe I can." She glanced at her handiwork—the lumpy patches of dark green over my floor.

I'd keep the feature. No use spending energy on changing something for no reason. Even though the greenery looked more like a meadow than the wilds, there was something unpredictable about it that I liked. Not that I liked unpredictability. I didn't. I liked when the sirens, prisoners, vampires, spirits, servants, and everyone else acted as they were supposed to. When *I* acted as I was supposed to. But here was a small concession to the part I rarely let myself indulge.

My shadow self agreed. Finally, something we could agree on besides the supremely unhelpful observation of Persephone's beauty. Every chance it got, the shadow drew my attention to the curve of her neck or the smoothness of her skin...

This was why I rarely drank, and when I did, it was always alone. Less chance of my inner chaos affecting somebody else.

I paced to a far window. I needed space. Staring out the window, I raked a hand through my hair.

"I'm not in the habit of apologizing," I said, "but I'm sorry I have to keep you here." And I was. She deserved a happier existence, and her presence kept throwing my focus out of alignment.

"I understand," she whispered.

Her answer hit me forcefully. I spun to face her again. "No, you were right to be angry."

Seeing her light dim day after day as she failed to catch human spirits hardened like a stone in my stomach. Despite her attempts to stand up for herself—against me, an exceptionally bold choice—she had no choice here but to do what I said. It wasn't fair to her.

What if she wanted to obey us? said the shadow, drawing my attention to the huge bed downstairs.

I bit back a growl. There were a thousand reasons that wasn't a good idea, even though my cock was starting to think otherwise. I recited them to myself.

One, she was my employee. My employee taken from her home and strongly urged into service.

Two, because of that, she had no way to deny me if I insisted. I'd never put someone in a position where they couldn't choose.

Three, if I gave in, all I'd be able to think about would be Persephone. My realm would suffer from my lack of attention. I was nothing if not obsessive. Right now, my realm commanded my focus.

Four, my limited sexual history—ancient history now—demonstrated loudly that my proclivities ran much darker than she'd be able to handle.

She was breakable, and this place would break her. That, or I would. The very thought brought bile to the back of my throat.

But look at her eyes when she looks at you, my shadow self hissed. *She wants you to take her, to bare her to you, to dominate her. We can take and take and take.*

My dick bulged painfully against my pants.

Shut up! Fucking lech.

I felt a sly smile in response.

"I'm glad you've discovered this breakthrough," I said, keeping my tone distant. I remained near the window, while she blocked the exit down to the ground floor.

A dimple appeared in one of her cheeks, unsure but proud. My stomach did an annoying flip, but the drink—drinks, plural, before she'd arrived—were rising to my head.

"I need the help." The words were out before I gave them permission.

My shadow self hissed. It didn't like when I showed vulnerability either. If I could have glared at him, I would have.

"The workers can clearly use it at the docks," I revised. That phrasing felt safer, somehow.

I shouldn't trust Persephone with anything personal. I barely knew her. Yet, looking at her now, it was hard to imagine she would use any confidence I shared against me.

Even half-hard, my mind churned out idiocy.

"Yes, they do," Persephone said. "I just wish it didn't have to be me. You need an army of people to help the humans! How do you manage it? I think I'd crack." The look in her eyes was so honest my breath caught. I had brought her here against her will and she was concerned about me?

Suddenly, the urge to spill all my thoughts rose like a tidal wave to the back of my tongue. I adjusted the neck of my collared shirt to buy myself the seconds it took to swallow them back down. "I wish it didn't have to be you either. You're too innocent for this work. This kind of thing..." When her expression soured, I took a couple steps forward over the new turf. I wasn't explaining myself well. "It's not for everyone. It demands things of you. Impossible things. A few of us have to bear impossible burdens so the rest don't feel them. I would have liked to put you in the latter category, but we don't have the luxury."

"I'm not asking to be babied," she shot back.

My speech had been smooth, conciliatory, hadn't it? "That's not what I'm saying."

"Isn't it? 'I'm too innocent for this work'?" Her blue eyes flashed.

I only wanted the sirens' powers to rub off on her, not their temper too. "That isn't what I meant," I said, voice lowering.

"Then what did you mean, Lord Hades?"

"Not that you should be babied, but protected from the fucking horrible realities here."

Her eyelashes fluttered once at my language.

A smirk curved my lips. "There," I said. "I'm immensely, *fucking* proud of the Far Realm, but it also has horrors. Dead human bodies piled at the docks with no one to catch their spirits are only one example. You shouldn't have to see that."

"What other horrors are there?" Her voice was thin but strong, like glass. She didn't break eye contact.

Asking me such brazen questions without fear was yet another example of her inexperience. But I sort of liked it. Her challenges felt good, like a stretch when it started to burn. Or a game. I rarely played games, but when I did, I won.

"Abaddon," I answered. "Gods who ate their own children, or who coaxed natural disasters."

Persephone's chest rose more quickly, but she didn't show any other signs of distress. She glared back with something like defiance.

I went on. "Tribes who mutilate anyone who enters their territory. Sprites who torture their enemies by sending them illusions fouler than any you could conjure in your mind."

She still gazed levelly at me, chin tipped up. Okay, I was a little surprised she displayed no reaction.

"Monsters so terrible that legend says a glimpse of them can drive a person mad." Those legends were bullshit, but I didn't add that. Most monsters were misunderstood. "Blood-sucking vampires who suck other things too. All together, on full moons." I let my meaning percolate in the air.

Persephone's pupils went wide, her cheeks flushed. Finally, a response. Was she... aroused?

What the fuck was I doing? I started by saying she was too innocent for any of this and promptly went on to try to corrupt her.

A claw slid down my sternum. *Not trying very hard.*

Fuck off.

My brain was fuzzy and blood was rushing to all the wrong parts. Persephone wasn't turned on by my litany of horrors.

"That's... I'm not... terrified of those things," she said stoutly, after a pause.

"It's natural if you are."

"Are you?"

"Not usually."

She arched a brow at me as if to say, *See?*

My gods, she needed to leave. Now. "Not usually" meant "yes

sometimes", and I was the fucking king of the Far Realm. I had no weakness because I could have no weakness. I was the most terrifying entity on the island. But Persephone tore off my desire to be terrifying. To her, I wanted to be protective, encouraging.

"Everyone's afraid of something," she said, laying a hand on my arm. Her touch sent alarms through my head. "If you weren't sometimes afraid, that would mean you didn't care."

I tried to pay attention without revealing how the soft pressure of her fingers stole most of my focus.

"I know you care about those humans at the docks, and I'll do my best to help you. Were…"

It took me a moment to realize she'd trailed off. "Hm?"

Her hand slipped off my arm. "Were there always monsters here? Before you arrived, I mean?"

My arm buzzed where her hand had been, but I could think more clearly now, even though she was looking at me with those godsdamned eyes. Fuck those drinks. "Some were," I answered. I sounded like myself. Smooth, in control. That was good. "Others, I took in. Stupid people didn't realize what they needed—some space, the right food…"

Persephone searched my face as if I were a thick novel she was rushing through. Her curiosity charmed me, but this shrewd attention on *me* felt unnerving.

I swiveled toward the window, gesturing out at the landscape. "There are areas dedicated to the most dangerous creatures, so they don't disrupt existing ecosystems. It's a delicate balance that's… not easy to maintain." From here, on a clear night like this, I could see the lights of thriving cities in the north, and the glint of moonlight on the ocean over the forests straight ahead. To the left, mostly in darkness, were the docks and the fortress.

"I can imagine," she said, standing beside me and looking out. Her strawberry scent mingled with the fresh grass. She made a little thoughtful noise as she devoured the sight of my kingdom. New to it, she didn't turn away or quail. She wanted more.

Unbidden visions of me giving her *more* tore through my thoughts. I'd force more noises out of her, make her pant and beg and whimper for more. She was under me, her hair sweat-soaked as she bit out the word she wouldn't say—"Fuuuck!"

"No time for a tour," I said, striding back toward the steps. I didn't look back when I added sharply, "Except that rusty colored dome you see if you look right? That's Abaddon. The prison can kill you. If I find you there again, you'll wish I hadn't." Whiskey and discomfort about what *might* have happened to her at the prison wall twisted my ordinarily cold demeanor into something cruel. Cruelty had many uses, but now regret lanced right behind the words.

I smoothed my shirt as I trotted lightly down the spiral steps and out to the main door of my suite. I yanked it open. "Marzanna!"

She approached in seconds, a ghostly apparition of flowing white and jagged black. "Yes, my lord?"

"Escort Persephone to her room in the fortress. She found the prison this evening and is terribly shaken by the experience."

Marzanna's dark eyes widened for a moment. "Yes, Lord Hades."

I risked a brief look at Persephone as she joined Marzanna.

Her forehead wrinkled, though I couldn't tell what emotion caused that look. It was something intense, yet confused.

Hopefully, I didn't wear the same expression on my face.

Denial was futile now. I liked this goddess. I wanted her. And just as surely, I knew I couldn't have her.

Because, beneath her dress, her skin was dotted with the shadow's bruises.

❧ 19 ❧

PERSEPHONE

I almost didn't feel the driving sheets of cold rain the next day. My body and mind had absorbed so much they had gone numb, spiraling and spiraling and spiraling around the bloodthirsty sirens who believed in me, grass responding to my power and spreading from under my palms, shadow creatures near evil walls, and Hades.

Always Hades.

My thoughts ended abruptly with him every time. From the moment the shadow creature had thrown me roughly at his feet, something felt different. Maybe it was because we were in his private chambers. The idea brought heat to my cheeks. But, more than that, I returned to his confession that he feared some of his subjects.

Why had he admitted that to *me*? Hades was the Eight Realms' most powerful god, yet he'd shown me a bare sliver of vulnerability. I saw it flash before he put on the impenetrable façade he usually wore.

Another crack in that ice-cold exterior shone through when

I covered his floor with lush green life. He wasn't angry. He was impressed.

I swiped hair out of my eyes. My pink dress was already soaked through to the skin. The scent of wet seaweed coated the air.

Until Hades' abrupt order for me to leave, I almost imagined...

No, that was stupid.

In the moment, though, Hades had softened. The lines in his brow relaxed. It was as though his knife-sharp glance became unarmed. The pit of my stomach had dropped low, making me squeeze my thighs together. Covertly, of course. I couldn't let him see that our proximity left my skin fizzing and my mouth dry and... other parts very wet.

Mother always said that gods and men only wanted to take advantage of girls like me. I wasn't a young girl anymore, but the warnings rang in my ears as surely as if I were. Everyone knew Thenios and other deathless ones sought pleasure wherever they could. But Hades? No story claimed that. He stood apart from the others. Untouchable and impressive. Cruel in his efficiency. Achingly beautiful.

But last night, I'd seen more—the effort it took to run a kingdom like this, and the care he had for his subjects.

I really liked his room. It smelled like minty winter nights when shelter was promised. It had stars and a pool and high-rising bookshelves and, through the archway, a huge circular bed with black sheets. Just like I'd imagined.

I blinked. No need to go on imagining Hades and his bed at all. He showed me a little bit of himself last night, but, just as quickly, he'd snapped back to the calculating ruler I knew. This was his version of kindness, not attraction.

I was the one getting drawn into a fantasy. Hades, god of the dead, certainly wasn't falling for a minor goddess who could make flowers grow.

Chastising myself, I reached the dock. Marzanna hadn't needed to lead me for several days. I realized the first time I found the way myself that there was actually a greenhouse attached to the fortress behind the steep staircase. I hadn't had an opportunity to sneak inside and see what grew there. The memory of the manticore left me unsure about wandering around the castle alone.

There was the pile of bodies, with shadowy figures walking lightly atop if with their lamps, singing, clipping hair. Drakaina was nowhere in sight. I'd gotten more used to the snake goddess, but she still carried a sense of dread with her that was hard to shake.

I closed my eyes. *Remember the plain. Remember Hades' chamber. Remember you are a goddess!*

With a long, inhale dribbly with rain, I opened my eyes and strode forward. The first human I encountered had clearly been killed in the Twins' war. A sure sword thrust cut a straight line of blood just below the heart. Musty copper filled my nose and I snuffed it out. If I spent too long dwelling on details, fixating on how dead this man was, I might lose my nerve.

I am a goddess.

The man was blond, his hair cut raggedly. His large nose was kind of cute. I could picture him as a child, running across sandy fields.

He deserved an afterlife. And I would give it to him.

I pushed his green tunic up and placed my palm over the exposed wound. This time, I didn't dig inside the body for life. There was none, just blood congealing and organs cooling down. But below him, in the land itself, and in the ocean and the sky above, there was life. I called to it. Felt a surge.

My hand popped off his chest. I didn't want to turn him into a hill of grass, and I could feel the plants responding.

No, the life is for him, not the plants. To heal his body and catch his spirit.

I went more carefully, massaging the skin around the wound with my fingers. The action made me cringe, but I kept going, focusing on the threads that needed to re-knit themselves.

The body obeyed my touch. The skin closed. But life kept surging through me. There was more, I knew it, the very air knew it.

I reached above with my power.

And gasped. So much life swirled above us that I felt almost claustrophobic. Like a thick swarm of fireflies, but bigger, more nebulous, the spirits floated.

A grin spread across my face. There they were! The spirits waiting to be reunited with a body, or at least tethered to the Far Realm instead of floating aimlessly into the ether. I sensed all of them.

With a glance at my blond soldier, I reached up with one hand. Emotion clogged my throat and pricked hot at my eyes.

Then I closed my fist and slammed it down beside the body.

The ground shook. The fog of spirits tore away like an awning, letting in clear moonlight.

"The spirit awaits,
the moon and tide rise.
Gather again
before the glow dies."

The Singers' verse faltered, breathless, as everyone paused.

A demi-god from the dock broke the sacred hush by unceremoniously tossing another corpse on the pile.

I stood. "Treat those bodies with respect," I snapped, surprising myself.

"We're doing what we can," he grumbled carelessly. "No time to give them all a funeral. We wouldn't have time for anything else."

I closed my fist again. Then a great stirring, like a wave, rumbled among the pile. Even the insolent dock worker turned back to see what was happening.

I already knew what was happening. I felt it the moment I stretched my power toward the spirits and sensed them all above me.

I, Seph from Kantharos, could save them all.

"Separate them," I ordered, dragging the blond man from the group by his legs as he started to stir. The Singers and dock workers jumped to attention as the mass heaved. Salvageable bodies had recaptured their spirits. Around the base of the pile, ghostly figures multiplied. Men, women, children, even figures that were undoubtedly demi-gods.

The workers obeyed. No one would want to regain consciousness in such a horrendous state. The least we could do is make sure they had space to move.

I dropped the soldier's legs. His eyes fluttered open. "Hi," I said with a smile. Tears coursed down my cheeks, joining the rain.

A line formed between his brows as he gazed first at me, then right, then left. "Is this... the Far Realm?"

I beamed and nodded.

He sat up. "Then where...?"

A small spirit, milky and glowing, careened into him. I would have guessed that spirits would float through objects, but this one had enough force to knock the man sideways. Laughing, crying, embracing each other, the two huddled together. The spirit was a little girl, I saw now, with hair that used to be dark like mine. I heard them whisper something about pancakes, like it was a secret. The man cupped the girl's face and kissed her forehead.

I needed to help detangle more bodies, separating the healed from the unhealable. But first, I turned away from the little family, crouched, covered my face with my hands, and wept.

❧ 20 ❧

PERSEPHONE

I bit back a squeal when my shift ended. It was all joy. Yes, I had to move mangled corpses. Yes, I was soaking from the rain. Yes, it was chaotic with so many disoriented humans toddling around, gaping at the surroundings, asking questions, searching for loved ones. But *damn*, it was satisfying!

My power had reunited someone's spirit with his body. Not only that, but it had imbued the ground or the air nearby with that same power. Spirits solidified, returning instead of fading away. The bodies that could still be used housed their old lives again. Or afterlives, I supposed.

Limbs creaked. Rags were brought out to daub away wet bloodstains. Marzanna spearheaded the effort to guide the human spirits away from the docks to the cover of the trees. From somewhere, a tent was put up to shelter them from the rain. Even the ghosts huddled under it, as if they would get wet.

I cried off and on all day. Mostly from joy, amazement, that all these people could have an afterlife now, and that I had helped that happen. Even new bodies brought to the spot instantly rose to their feet or wafted up like a cloud of cream in a cup of tea to materialize in a different form. But there were sad moments too. A woman realized her arm was missing and now she'd never have it back. Several people couldn't find their loved ones. One man found a comrade among the corpses, whose spirit wasn't among the ghosts or in the Singers' vessels. He was gone, and we left the man to clutch at the ragged remains of his friend.

A hand touched my shoulder. It was Marzanna, looking fierce as ever, her pale face and black lips phantom-like in a place already crowded with ghosts. "You should return, Seph."

I hadn't noticed I was shivering until she touched me.

"You've stayed beyond your time, and you should celebrate the good you've done for us here." Her unearthly black eyes bored into me with new intensity. Maybe this was how Marzanna expressed thanks. There went her lips, lifting in the thinnest of smiles. On her, however, a smile meant everything. "That power of yours..." she mused.

I glanced down at my hands. Even now, I could hardly believe it myself. "Thank you for believing I could do it."

"I didn't know you could do this. I thought you were a lesser goddess." No hint of apology graced her words, just... pride or... awe, even.

I blushed. "Is there a place set up for them to stay for now?"

"We're finding them accommodations until we can set up something more permanent. We don't have many prepared areas for the great number of human spirits coming to us."

"Does Hades know what happened?" I asked. He would be

so excited. He cared deeply for the spirits and never doubted my ability, even when I did.

"Lord Hades has not yet received the news," she replied.

Should I have called him "Lord Hades" instead of just "Hades"? Marzanna gave the barest quirk of her eyebrow that said she noticed how familiar I was growing toward him. Well, not familiar, exactly. No one was truly familiar with the great Lord Hades. Still, we had become something. Acquaintances, perhaps even friends after last night...

"Can I tell him?" I asked.

Marzanna inclined her head. Rainwater slithered down her antlers.

I grinned and travelled through the air toward his palace. I paid attention when Marzanna had brought me back to the fortress last night. I could find it again without doing something foolish like running into the god-prison.

Darkness. Rain-soaked pine needles.

Darkness. A swift-flowing river.

Darkness. A break in the gray clouds.

Darkness. A castle that looked like fairy tales and cozy nights and forbidden fantasies all rolled into one. All the promise of the night. Its spires and enchanting suspended bridges looked like an ebony confection. And the finery of it. It was enormous, even by god standards, radiating wealth and beauty and importance. Hades was right to scoff at my assumption that I'd been staying in his palace all along.

One more jump through the air landed me at the door. Some enchantment prevented me from entering. Typically, there were rooms designated for that kind of thing, for security's sake. Knowing Hades, he might not have one at all.

I pounded at the door. Drops flew from my wet clothes, although it wasn't raining here. I must have looked wild, but my news was too important to wait. Shocking that no one had sent word already. But we were all so stunned and busy, no one had time to take a breath, much less travel halfway across the Far Realm to relay a message.

The shadow creature had dropped me off directly in Hades' room, I remembered. Why did it have such exclusive access? Maybe it had grabbed me on Hades' orders and was told to bring me to him.

Something prickled in the back of my mind.

"Would you like to know what my power is?"

When I'd first seen the violent creature, its dark shape had shaken some memory loose, as if I'd seen it before. It was man-shaped. Deadly. With a hint of seething elegance...

One gold-veined double door opened, dashing my thoughts away. Two figures looked out, male and female.

The female was beautiful, dark-skinned, with sharp, alluring eyes. She wore a large green hat or scarf that seemed to move slightly as if something under it were alive. Her fingertips ended in sharp claws.

Beside her was the male, equally tall, slim and pale, with dark hair and dark wings neatly folded behind him. He stood with a preternatural stillness that made it easy to envision him exploding with movement.

Both of them would fit nicely into the naughty books I liked to read. Their loveliness paired with the sense of danger filled the air thickly like a scent. But I refused to be intimidated.

"I'm here to see Hades," I gasped.

"He's holding court," said the male in a silky voice. A trace of pointed teeth showed through when he opened his mouth. Was this one of the vampires Hades said were so frightening yesterday?

"Where?" I asked.

The female observed me doubtfully. I knew I looked a wreck, and I didn't care. I probably smelled a wreck too. "In his throne room," she answered, as if it should be obvious.

I pursed my lips. "Please, sir, my lady..." I faltered. "I have incredibly exciting news to share with him. Please let me in."

The green fabric on her head writhed again.

The male pivoted to stand aside. "I shall escort you."

I exhaled, following him inside. Normally, this would be scary, but the bubble of amazement I felt from today wouldn't dim. Even a vampire and a dangerous goddess couldn't keep me down.

The palace was as magnificent on the inside as it was on the outside. My gut coiled with longing. It was the ache of loving a place so much I already missed it, even though I hadn't left.

It wasn't my reading shed full of blooms. This was the other side of me, the side that liked beautiful wildness even when it meant black flowers mixed in with the bright ones. The lobby we passed felt grand and familiar at once.

I hadn't known my spirit looked like this. Soaring, black, bursting with pomegranates and peonies the color of mulberry wine, sapphire-studded waterfalls splashing into waiting jars gathered by goblin children, long-tailed birds white as spirits, thick rugs depicting the night sky...

I hungered for more. Was insatiable.

The humans were lucky to live in a place with such beauty

in it. Too bad their first glimpse was the docks. Happily, Drakaina had stayed away today, taking care of her unsavory business out of sight of the dead. She would have sent more than a few of them back into the boats to try their luck on the Stygian Sea.

"Here we are." The vampire gestured through another door flanked by guards with hideously deformed bear-like faces, but with an endearing determination and competence in their eyes.

Faint voices sounded within. Then a response. Hades' voice.

"Join the line." The vampire licked the corner of his lips as I stepped through into the throne room. I should have feared him, but I felt so powerful. I *was* so powerful. And my power had saved the dead humans.

The throne room was larger than the lobby by far. And the vampire was right. A long line stretched nearly the length of the room. All manner of human and deathless being and creature waited their turn to speak to the figure on the throne.

Just inside the door was a small footbridge of pure obsidian, like the columns in Hades' chambers, arching over a stream of dark water. Hades himself occupied the far end. At the three other sides of the long chamber stood strong, naked women, each holding a spear. Their bodies were twisted half into bird shape. There was a mesmerizing kind of ferocity about them, though. Hades' guards, I guessed.

Why did he need guards at all? He seemed powerful enough on his own.

The next suppliant stepped forward, a goat-legged demigod. With head bowed, he poured a cup of wine out before Hades' feet.

Upon his black throne, backlit by torches, Hades echoed his palace—all nightmare and fantasy. His fine suit cut a menacing silhouette. His fingers upon the skull-and-black-rose armrests moved with restless grace. Stiffness in his shoulders suggested he was tired or frustrated by giving this audience for so long. But despite the shadows, his gray eyes lanced out pure as a light, fearsome intelligence in them.

My breath hitched. I'd stopped breathing.

His eyes met mine. They flared, with surprise or anger or something else, I didn't know. Intensity was all I sensed clearly.

I cleared my throat. I didn't know what these other beings were here to say, but I doubted any of them could beat my news. "Lord Hades," I said, voice carrying in the echoey room. I grinned. "I did—"

"Persephone." His voice cut like a knife. My stomach dropped. His hand sliced outward, its meaning clear. Get to the back of the line.

I screwed up my forehead. Hades was the one who insisted I had enough power to reunite the human spirits to their bodies to offer them an afterlife. He knew how important my message could be. *Eternally* important to so many!

For a second, I considered shouting my news anyway. But doing that in front of so many people wouldn't go over well. Hades wasn't the most feared god of the Eight Realms for nothing. He'd punish me somehow.

The injustice of it! I wouldn't have attempted to skip the line if I didn't think my information was worth sharing this minute.

And the way he just... dismissed me. It was like that moment last night when his eyes had shuttered. That glimpse beneath the surface cut off. I felt like I'd been caught stealing, looking at something I shouldn't. But why not? Was it so important that no one knew Hades had a heart?

I created a dripping line from the door, across the little bridge, to the back of the line.

I didn't need the vampire Evard's soft command as he opened the door or the sound of a footstep to know Persephone had entered the throne room. My entire being locked onto her the moment she entered, soaking wet and exultant.

She took a wondering moment to scan the room before she smiled at me.

Even dripping with rainwater, she looked fresher and more beautiful than anyone else there. I struggled to think of anyone I'd *ever* seen who looked lovelier. Her pink dress stuck to her tan legs. Everywhere were hints of the wildness I'd sensed beneath her submissive surface. Now she glowed, ferociously joyful, long black hair crazy, blue eyes luminescent.

Something in me ballooned as if a force pulled me bodily to her. It wasn't my shadow self, though he noticed her too. With the snarl of a startled dog, it bucked inside me.

Look, look, look! it—he—said. The rest was incomprehensible and hungry noises. They nearly escaped from my mouth.

Control. I had no control.

All I wanted was Persephone. She'd ensnared me, wet and triumphant like this. Her power had worked at the docks. That was clear. Damn all these other people.

No. No. It was good they were here.

My thoughts hardly functioned. My brain, my skin, my balls, all yearned toward her. I wanted her news, wanted her alone, wanted to tease more joy from her...

I knew this yanking in my belly. Obsession. Though the onset had never felt so rampant.

Fuck, I'd been afraid of this.

I clamped my teeth down and took a breath.

I was Hades, god of the fucking dead, and I could control myself. I wasn't a creature—not completely—and I wouldn't act like my brother Thenios when he found someone with less power. Persephone was good, better than me, in kindness and that sort of thing, anyway. She was innocent and didn't want to be dominated by a cruel god.

Wine splashed my sandaled feet. I didn't look away from Persephone.

But I should.

"Lord Hades," she called out. "I did—"

"Persephone." I gestured fiercely. She had to follow the order of my court, just like anyone else. Desperation flooded my veins. If I let her trample on decorum, the rest of that thread would unravel. I'd give her more license to do anything she pleased. Others would demand the same exceptions. The fragile ecosystem here would totter.

At that moment, I hated being king.

Her shoulders sloped and her grin evaporated. My mouth

opened to say something else, something that would reverse the effect I had on her. But I could give no ground. I dug my fingers into the armrest of the throne. My fourth finger found an eye socket. Years had taught me that if I found myself gripping the eye of Tantalus, I needed to relax.

"Lord Hades," said someone near my feet.

Only centuries of reining in my shadow self prevented him from ripping out of me to tear apart the fawn for speaking.

I took a steadying breath. His heavy accent told me he'd learned my name in the common tongue, but it wasn't a language he understood. I sifted my mind for Hingat, his native dialect. "Tell me, why have you come?"

Horns glinted through a mess of curly bronze hair as he bowed his head. "Your magnificence, my family's land has been encroached upon by marauding lycans. We cannot withstand them. My littlest, Hazel, lost a leg a few months back. We have stood up to them, but we haven't been successful."

"Where?"

"The border of the Aridian forest and the Northlands, my lord."

Lycans would rather die than be caged, so giving them a place to live that didn't threaten others was devilishly tricky.

"What's your name?"

"Oh," he responded, flustered, "it's... my name is Birch."

"Birch, I will send the shadow there in two weeks. Stay in your houses. The lycans won't harm you again."

The fawn quivered at the mention of my greatest weapon. I didn't intend to kill all the wolf-beasts. No one was immune to a threat that could leave them all as shivering piles of viscera within seconds. Fear, and maybe one demonstration, would do it. Add it to the list.

"Thank you, my lord, Lord Hades. You're very kind."

"Look after Hazel."

"I will, Lord Hades." He bowed and moved aside.

A family of demi-gods approached next. I recognized them instantly by their red scaly skin. I'd granted them sanctuary after the human queen of Kantharos had asked the realm's goddess to destroy them. No one really enjoyed their company, even here, but being creepy as fuck didn't mean you didn't have a right to exist. All three of them required blood for survive, and the youngest had a nasty habit of exploding. Orderly, uptight Kantharos couldn't have beings like this running around, ruining everything and exploding at inconvenient moments.

The mother poured the drink offering.

But behind her, at the back of the line, Persephone stirred. Her arms were crossed over her chest and her blue eyes stared at me.

Persephone was from Kantharos. Had she ever heard of this misfit family?

They were saying something. "...wanted to thank you for letting us stay here."

I blinked. "You're welcome. The Far Realm is a home for those without one," I said automatically. Of all the things I expected her to say, this wasn't it.

Rumors of their land disputes and arguments and job reassignments filtered to me now and then. Common sense told me to anticipate a complaint, not thanks.

All three of them bowed and laid something else at the foot

of the throne. A gift. The nearest Fury peeled away from the wall where she stood guard and gathered it.

I let my features relax. "I accept your thanks gladly."

The exploding youth gave a toothy smile. His father roughly patted him on the shoulder as though he had overstepped.

I held public court like this once a week. It was exhausting. If I didn't consider it so important, I would have stopped long ago. Anyone was welcome. Deathless came to ask favors, humans to pay their respects, creatures to make complaints. Each approached the throne one at a time. Rarely were there any disturbances, and, if there were, I loosened the leash on my other self and made everyone behave.

I'd learned twenty different languages to communicate with all my refugees and spirits and workers and native groups. Latest was Qa-a-ka. Devilishly hard. Mostly clicks and rasps. The troll I commanded to teach me knew when to make a swift exit. At least now I could talk about storm suns and quarrying and prophecy. You know, all the most important points of conversation.

Anyway, none of that mattered right now.

This session was particularly difficult to get through, because all my concentration focused on listening and responding, listening and responding. All I wanted was to hear Persephone, but, other than my growing fixation, nothing made her more important than these others. Not even her job at the dock.

That mantra repeated in my mind until I felt the ruts like brutal grooves made by pacing feet. My mind was sore, my shadow restless, by the time Persephone finally approached the throne. She had no wine.

"Lord Hades." Her hard expression thawed now that she could finally speak. She let her arms fall to her sides, but her forehead still wrinkled with annoyance. Couldn't say I blamed her. But I had to be fair to my subjects and maintain the equilibrium—the order—that held this kingdom together.

"Persephone."

She'd stopped correcting me.

She likes when you say her full name like that. It sends a shiver down her spine and a throbbing to her—

A scowl made it halfway across my features before I schooled them again. Persephone didn't know the internal battle I fought every day. "You said you had news."

"I do. May I speak?" The clipped question didn't sound like her. It wasn't sweet and curious and earnest. It was defiant.

In front of everyone.

I can punish her. We can both punish her for this insolence. You are the most powerful god in all the Realms.

Shut the fuck up and let me handle this.

"You may." My body felt too rigid, my voice too cold.

"My power worked at the docks." Her breathing kind of... released. All that pent-up excitement was flooding out again. It reached her eyes first, then the rest of her face, before she said quickly, "It worked, Hades. You were right. I didn't just reunite one spirit to its body. I... I saved all of them."

I froze. "All of them."

"Every spirit. Even the ones who came in later. It's something about that spot. It has life in it now or something. It's more than I ever thought would happen." Tears glistened in her sapphire eyes. Gasps and shuffles around the room.

A storm of emotion blew through me. Hope had let me down too many times. Was this even possible? Did those poor dead humans finally have a real chance at immortality here instead of only nothingness and decay?

Hope is a bitch. Don't trust her.

I swallowed, realized I was leaning forward. "Send someone there to see if this is true," I snapped to one of my attendants.

"It is true." That aggrieved look knitted her brow again.

"You've been wrong before."

"All the spirits are there. Go see," she said. "They need somewhere to stay. The Singers are helping to orient them, but they shouldn't stay on that beach if we can help it."

If what she said was true, this was beyond my wildest imagining. And I couldn't help believing her. All day long, I sifted lie from fact. Persephone had never lied to me. She shone clear as truth itself.

I knew she could heal bodies and coax their spirits back. But this...? Never.

This meant Persephone was one of the most powerful goddesses I'd ever met.

My cock throbbed. Powerful and good, solving this godsawful problem for thousands of humans... Hunger pressed against my ribcage. I narrowed to one thing: Persephone.

Yes, growled my other self, vibrating with excitement.

I took in her slight flush, her soft mouth, her wet hair, her hands capable of unthinkable healing.

This feeling wasn't some fluttery infatuation. It was pain.

I had to confirm her claim. I was still king. I had a job to do.

Stupid, empty words. But I made myself say them. "I'll personally confirm it. Thank you. That's all."

A rock clogged my throat at the glacial distance I created with the dismissal.

Fucking shit, this was bad.

She'd performed a miracle. Two miracles, maybe. I, always hanging onto control with a tight fist, felt it rip from my grasp. Now *she* dominated *me*.

I had to get out, get out, get out. I could hardly remember why. But the raging darkness inside shouldn't be this aroused. Chaos lurked at the edge of everything and couldn't spill across my kingdom.

Not again.

In the first years of my reign, Abaddon had broken, destroyed most of my population. My shadow destroyed even more as he forced Typhon and the other monstrous gods back into their prison. Only Drakaina and a few others knew, but it lurked in my memory like a disease. It could happen again. And when it did, it would be my fault.

I couldn't lose my grip on control now, not as Abaddon was starting to crack...

Persephone's brows scrunched down. She gave me one last look. I saw how much I hurt her, how she felt belittled and angry.

My shadow stirred, panting, straining to get out.

No! I held myself together from one breath to the next.

The door closed behind Persephone. The next person

approached, but I had no more room in my head for anything else.

The open session was over.

22

PERSEPHONE

I left the throne room with hot eyes. My damp clothes were starting to feel chilly. Adrenaline because of my raw power had warmed me, but now began to wear off.

Hades didn't believe me.

Had I done something to make him doubt my word? All he'd said about how I underestimated myself, that gleam in his eye when I'd summoned velvet green grass in his chambers... I was powerful. I'd *saved* people today, and it still wasn't enough for him.

I hadn't realized until now how part of my excitement at the docks had been to see Hades' reaction when he heard my news. A dim part of my mind had conjured stupid pictures from my books, casting me as Esmeralda and him as Dracon. His eyes—so similar to the heart-stopping glance I'd imagined—would sharpen with astonishment, then fill with hunger.

I burned thinking of my daydreams now. I would never be enough for Hades.

He was not only frighteningly powerful and heart-wrenchingly beautiful, but a just ruler to his people. Watching him deal with the variety of beings and their requests as each approached the throne was like watching a symphony. Each person had his full attention. Maybe that was why he had guards, to watch everyone else. His air of authority never wavered, but his gestures and voice did, depending on the supplicant. I heard him speak two languages I didn't recognize with an ease that sent an icicle of pleasure down my back. The desperate were comforted, the arrogant sent low.

I was a storm of emotion by the time it was my turn. It made me act like someone else. Or maybe it was the piece of me I'd stuffed down too long—the piece tired of being dismissed like a child, controlled, ignored in high company. I'd proven to myself and others what I was capable of.

Hades had conducted the affairs of his kingdom beautifully —so beautifully I ached—until he got to me. I was still little Persephone to him. I thought he'd believe me, at least.

A bitter chuckle escaped my mouth as I charged out the vaulting front door of the palace. I didn't want to go back to my room. I wanted to remind myself that Hades wasn't right about me.

Here, he was my king, but I controlled my own life. I didn't need his approval.

I knew it was true, but that didn't make it hurt any less. Stepping ferociously through the air, I headed back in the direction of the docks. I'd check to see if my power still lingered while I wasn't there. Were human spirits still being caught in that spot I'd imbued with magic?

Marzanna spied me first. Despite the rain, I could see her clearly in the glow of ghosts being herded away from the beach by Singers. Her unearthly features grew alien as she looked at me. Sometimes I forgot she was what humans would call a monster. But then something would go blank in her eyes, and her antlers would glint in the moonlight.

"You told Lord Hades?" she asked, another question behind that one.

Faintly, behind her, someone still sang the chanting song. This time, though, it sounded like habit—something to pass the time—instead of the reverent, insistent way they'd sung it before.

"Yes." I couldn't keep the bitterness from my tone. In a strange way, it soothed me to return to the place where I'd earned my greatest victory. Soon enough, Hades would see I was right.

"Was he not pleased?"

"He's very busy."

Marzanna's thin, black lips quirked. "The king is always busy, but surely he relishes this triumph. If your power holds, a great weight will be lifted from his shoulders."

"Has it held? Are the spirits tethered before they disappear, like before?"

Marzanna smiled. For some reason, the very creepiness of the smile made me even more proud of myself. Even this strange goddess found my strength impressive. "Yes. Every human drawn from a boat has healed or coalesced into a stable spirit. Some are heading to the Singers' quarters, others to the fortress."

Raindrops streamed down my hair. Suddenly, I hugged Marzanna. The goddess stiffened. This probably never happened to her, but the day had been so long, and had felt so big, and I had so many emotions I didn't know what to do with. Despite the odd way we met and the terrible things we'd witnessed together, I was grateful for Marzanna. She was never ruffled. She brought me yummy food and naughty books. She cared for me in her own way.

"Exhaustion has overtaken you," she declared, gently peeling me off her. "You must rest."

I didn't feel like resting, but she was right. Sighing, I headed back across the sand to the fortress. Maybe I'd relax in a bath and try to sort out some of the gnarled string of what had happened today.

The sky grew more threatening as I neared the sea. Gray turned to black. A breeze turned into a lashing gale. It all felt fitting. If only I could duck into my home back in Kantharos to smell Mother's bread cooking while I prepared mushroom soup for supper.

What about the greenhouse, the small one attached to the fortress on the ground level? I'd wanted to see it. That sounded cozy, a return to something familiar. A few flowers, plants, or vegetables could soothe my soul.

At the thought, I longed for the smell of earth. That sounded better than a bath just now.

Thunder cracked overhead. I squeaked and started running. Torrents of freezing rain lashed down, chasing me inside.

I yanked open the door and shut it quickly behind me. I held onto the handle while I caught my breath and allowed warmth to fill me. Everything in here smelled heavy and green. My breath fogged the glass door. This was a manageable haven for my ability.

Exhaling, I fingered the plant on the shelf beside me. It still bobbed with the force of the wind as I'd opened the door. "Sorry," I whispered, coaxing it back to full life. It took no thought to do that, now. Just a touch. Even easier than before. Browning edges extended into moist green leaves of perfect shape. I added flowers here and there because I could. One by one. Like meditation, which I'd never done. The closest thing for me was reading and now this.

Rain pelted the glass relentlessly, melting the view of anything outside.

Another roar of thunder.

Then the door opened and closed again, now at the opposite end of the little greenhouse, a couple paces away from me.

I jerked my attention up. Hades met my eyes and scoffed in disbelief. The rain had slicked his hair, even his suit. I'd never seen him so disheveled. The wet shirt under his suit clung to his chest. Rivulets ran down his temples, making him look a little messy and, honestly, really, really good.

Between the night and the storm, it was dark, but lights from the castle bled in through the rain-spattered glass, edging the leaves around us and the planes of his shadowed face.

"Of course," he muttered.

I squared myself at him. "What are you doing here, Lord Hades? Were you looking for me?"

"No, I wasn't looking for you," he snapped, remaining by the door.

The greenhouse was small enough that, although we stood on opposite ends, a few steps away, we might as well have been pressed together.

"I was checking your work at the dock. One look and I knew your power had worked." This time, his voice came out more studied, elegant, as it usually did. Still with that bite of command, but without the vitriol that seemed to come out only around me.

We must have just missed each other at the wharf.

I searched his eyes for praise. That hint of admiration I'd seen in his quarters. But he looked away.

"It did, and it's still working, even when I'm not there," I said, trailing my hand through another pot of flowers. Beads of water dripped loudly from my dress to the floor.

"We have to find places for the spirits," he muttered.

Through my annoyance, I hurt for him. Everyone on this huge island depended on Hades, and the weight was crushing him. I saw it in the set of his forehead, the way wet tendrils of hair fell over his face as his gaze turned inward. Maybe he hadn't meant to be so sharp with me.

"There are a lot of humans on Kantharos," I said. "If you want, I can tell you what they like as far as their homes and food and everything. I'm sure you already have a lot of experience, but if it would be helpful..."

"No need for that." He raised his eyes to mine again. My heart kicked up at their intensity. Was he angry?

My compassion for him melted away. Hades had no right to be mad at me. He was the one who demanded that I help him. He couldn't use pride as a shield now to pretend I hadn't done just that.

"Why do you hate me so much?" I demanded. I doubted he would send me to Abaddon for asking impertinent questions. Maybe it was time to break the rules. At least then I'd have answers. I was a generally happy, hard-working person who kept to herself. Sure, the past few weeks had been incredibly hard, but I'd come through in ways I never thought I could. Why had I still not earned a crumb of respect from Hades? He should be thanking me.

"I don't hate you." But he said it dismissively, scowling as he slipped his hands in his pockets.

Emotion rose in my throat. "You do. You've been mean to me ever since the prison. I've done everything you asked."

His sharp features softened a fraction. "It's not that."

"Then what is it?"

He refused to meet my eyes. He was the king, but I couldn't help thinking he should still apologize for the way he'd treated me.

We stood in silence. Okay, he wouldn't tell me what he thought I'd done wrong. I crossed my arms, hating how beautiful he was and how he reminded me of stars and danger and late winter nights.

The longer I stood there in that frigid quiet listening to the driving rain, the more I sensed some of the plants slowly dying. Well, that was one thing I could fix. I couldn't force the god of the dead to be honest with me, but I could heal the leaves.

I uncrossed my arms and ran one hand over the nearest plant, a surprisingly tropical one that didn't belong here. It looked too wild. I wished I could free it, like some caged animal, so it wouldn't have to live out its days in this unforgiving land.

Hades watched me as I stroked the leaves, rooting out decay and replacing it with life. I was glad Hades was here to see it. *See,* I wanted to scream, *I'm not a failure. I am magic.* Coming to terms with my new power was disorienting enough without the push and pull of Hades' reactions—or lack of them.

I made my way down the shadowy shelf, feeling as I went, healing every broken leaf, root, and stem. He didn't move as I got closer to where he stood near the door. Fine. I'd work around him.

When I reached the end of one side and switched to the other, I accidentally bumped his back. He hissed in a breath.

I tried to ignore the heat rising to my face.

"Stop." The order came so unexpectedly that I didn't immediately obey. He took two steps and barred my way with an arm. "Stop."

I glared at him. This was too much. He didn't want me to heal his plants? I stared in his face while I made a flower bloom, big and bright, right where it didn't belong. It was vivid pink, even in the dark.

Hades didn't move his arm, glowering down at me. The heat of his breath gusted in my face.

For the first time since I entered the greenhouse, anxiety bubbled up inside me. We were alone.

Something shifted in the air between us. His frown lost its hard edge, his brilliant eyes darted over my face, down to my mouth, and lower...

The chill I'd felt a moment ago was utterly gone. My cheeks flamed. That sinful mouth with its carved edges drew my gaze. It went sensuously slack.

I was like a leaf in a whirlpool, powerless against a stronger force. Here was the Hades I'd glimpsed behind the ice-sharp veneer. The one I yearned for so fiercely, it was as if I'd lost part of my soul in him and needed to dig it out.

What was happening? I had to back up, to move away. This was *Hades*, the god that other gods feared.

But he wasn't moving either.

My stomach knotted as I forced myself to look back in his eyes. When his met mine again, he broke away with a curse, running one hand through his hair, his bicep flexing with the motion.

"Fuck," he repeated. "I can't..."

Between his hair that looked sleep-wild and his broken sentences, Hades wasn't himself. Not the self-assured monarch he'd been in the throne room an hour ago. His wicked poise dimmed into something new.

I watched, unsure.

"The... power is working," he said, his voice clipped. "If that continues, then you... may go back. To Kantharos."

I wasn't sure what to expect, but it wasn't that. "What?"

"You can go back home." His eyes shuttered, the gray going black like the sky.

"Just like that, you're dismissing me?" I couldn't have explained why I was so upset. I wanted to go home, to see Mother and the other gardeners again, to read in my little shed. But the thought of leaving this savage place for somewhere tame, another land where people wouldn't take my power seriously, soured my stomach.

"You did what I asked you to do." His hands clasped behind his back. "You did it well. I'll arrange for someone to take you back."

It wouldn't even be Hades himself? I frowned. "No," I said. "You can't just bring me here and toss me out when you're done with me." Angry tears bit at my eyes.

"Don't tell me what I can't do."

"You've told me plenty of times!"

That was it. I'd done it. I talked back to the god of the dead.

His jaw flexed in the darkness. "This is a good time for you to leave."

Breath caught in my throat. I didn't want to leave. I'd done miraculous things today and I felt more dangerous than I ever had. "I'm healing the rest of the plants," I whispered, beginning again.

From the corner of my eye, I saw his chest rise and fall more intensely as he stared at me.

A second ago, when he'd looked at me... It sounded ludicrous, but I saw desire there. Like I'd seen in his rooms.

Impossible.

"Persephone," he said, lower this time. Kinder and more careful. "You must leave."

"I'm sorry if I've been a burden, but after today—"

A humorless laugh burst from his mouth. "A burden! Yes, you've been a burden."

His outburst speared me through the heart. *Never enough, never enough...* I made an angry red poppy blossom in the planter. "Is this because I got close to the prison? I told you—"

"No! Obviously not!" He took a step toward me. Stopped, as if something physically prevented him from coming closer.

A half-frenzied gleam glinted in the dark. He was tousled and ragged and not himself. My body stood at attention.

"Then what?" I asked softly.

"I can't afford to be distracted," he said. "I can't afford the time, the thought—none of it. Hell, even this storm!" He ground his teeth, his jawline getting even sharper. He narrowed his focus on me. "I cannot afford to be distracted, but I have been, which is why you need to stay out of my way."

I struggled to keep up with what he was saying. Was he saying what I thought he was saying? "Am I... distracting you?"

He growled, advancing on me. "Yes, Persephone, yes! That's what I'm saying. Don't come near me. Don't follow me."

He had followed *me,* but I didn't say that. I held my ground, my pulse spiking as his large form penned me in, muscled arms in wet sleeves a breath away from my waist. Leaves teased the back of my head.

"Don't talk to me. Don't do anything to make me think about you." But his mouth was already descending to mine. Hades' hot breath teased my mouth, and I surged up to meet his soft lips.

I'd imagined kisses a hundred ways, but not this wet, panting, rough, messy kind of kiss. The kind that knocked planters over and felt like an angry conversation. The kind with his hair dripping into my eye and a growl in my own throat I didn't know was there. Half a dozen times we started to pull away but couldn't bear it. Large, calloused hands squeezing my sides, my legs, my neck, and finally pushing me away so hard I grunted and almost fell after the shelf hit my back. Here and there, plants grew wild, huge and sprawling or clustered with blooms where they hadn't been before.

"No!" he rasped, pointing ferociously at me. "No. You have to leave."

I stood up straight, drawing my arms across my belly. "That wasn't my fault."

He pursed his lips. "No," he admitted, deflating a little. "I shouldn't have done that. I lost my head. It won't happen again."

But I wanted it to happen again. Right now.

When I didn't move, he arched a brow. We stood on opposite sides of the greenhouse again. "Persephone," he said softly, his face growing oddly pained, "you have to go. You were right. This place isn't good for you. This"—he waved a hand—"this is nothing."

It took a couple heartbeats to find the courage to say the question blazing in my mind. It still came out barely audible. "Does it have to be nothing?"

His expression deepened. Profound, ancient pain surfaced in his eyes a moment, like a reflection on water. "Yes," he answered. "This place is far from your family. You've done what you can here. You're meant for spring. Good, kind places. Not this. The Far Realm will eat you alive."

"It's tried, and I'm still here." The reminder bolstered my resolve. "I'm stronger than when I first got here."

A crooked smile ghosted over his face in the dark. "Not strong enough."

Maybe he was right. Wanting Hades would only end in pain for me if that was what he thought. "Fine," I said frostily. Pieces of my heart split into a thousand spidery cracks.

"That's not what I meant." He made a sound in his chest, like a deep, frustrated growl. "You, Persephone, are one of the most powerful goddesses I've ever seen." He wasn't flattering me. He believed it. And he tasted my name as if he were sucking butter off his fingers. My pulse throbbed between my legs.

"I mean you wouldn't survive me," he clarified. He leaned

back against the streaming glass, idly straightening his cuffs. On anyone else the gesture would have been an expression of total ease, but I could tell he was uncomfortable.

I waited for him to go on.

"I am not safe."

"Of course I know you aren't safe," I said. "But you've taken care of me."

"You said I was cruel to you." His distant tone was back again, complete with the slightly tilted chin. He had more command of himself, and a part of me grieved to see it. I hungered for the wildness in his eyes.

"You saved my life and believed in my abilities."

He waved his hand again as if that were nothing too. It struck me that he hadn't stepped through the air back to his palace. The wards that prevented me from traveling directly inside wouldn't apply to him. He was choosing to stay here with me.

"You protect the ones you care about," I persisted. "I understand if..." How could I say it? We'd shared a kiss—and what a kiss!—but I still couldn't voice the idea that Hades of the Far Realm wanted to be with me, however much he protested. "I understand if this can't work. That makes sense," I said quickly. "But I care about the human spirits. Let me help them find a place to enjoy their afterlife. And what if my power wears off?"

He scoffed drily. "It won't." He didn't look at me, but I could see his throat work.

A small smile crawled onto my face. He was sure. And he knew divine abilities. He must have sensed the truth somehow. I glanced down and chewed my lip, pleased.

"I never told you my ability," he said suddenly.

I jerked my head up.

He regarded me like one would an enemy.

"No," I agreed, burning to know. "What is it?"

He looked impossibly graceful and wild at once. His eyes glowed with focused determination. "That shadow that took you from the wall—it's me."

"You?" I frowned, uncomprehending.

He ran a hand through his mussed hair. "I can release it at will. There's nothing stronger in the Realms than the shadow when I let it fully off its leash."

A shiver ran through me. "You turn into it?"

"It's part of me. I remain and *usually* it stays inside, but it can separate bodily from me." He seemed to be struggling for words somewhat, which Hades rarely did. He was so self-assured.

I canted my head. "Why are you telling me this?"

His mouth made tiny, mesmerizing motions as he considered his answer. "Because you deserve to know. The shadow is not kind and the shadow is me."

I remembered the corpse of the creature outside my bedroom. How it had been torn apart just before Hades entered the room. How the shadow had disappeared in Hades' room right after he threw me down. How the shadow had looked familiar... The truth clicked into place.

Would it sound condescending if I assured him that he was still worthy of love? From the glint in his eye earlier, when I'd seen that bone-deep loneliness, I doubted he believed that.

I opened my mouth.

"I've given you at least three good reasons now to go back

home while you still can," he said, cutting me off before I could speak.

But I was done letting him cut me off. "I'm not afraid of the shadow."

"You should be."

"You said you have it under control."

His face contorted into a bitterly cynical shape. "Hard to pin the bastard down sometimes. Like now. Time to sleep. In the morning, you can go."

He strode forward on long legs, seized me by the arm, and the greenhouse disappeared. The air dried. The minty scent of Hades filled my nose.

I opened my eyes. We were outside my bedroom in the fortress.

Hades released my arm.

"Hades," I said quickly. Inside, his wet hair and suit looked even wilder. I didn't know what to say to him, but I wanted him to stay, even if it was just to talk. I wanted to know more about his other self, about his challenges in the Far Realm. I wanted to tell him how stifled I felt back home and how, here, I was starting to understand who I truly was.

I wanted to kiss him again.

I wanted more than that.

The feared god of the dead said I distracted him, was looking at me with an almost angry desperation.

"Get some sleep, Persephone."

I cracked open the door but didn't go inside. "What if... I refuse to go?" My question came out small as I looked up at Hades through lowered lashes.

My stomach flipflopped as he held my gaze, blood pumping

so forcefully through my veins that I felt choked. Hades' face was a mask. A devastatingly handsome mask, with the most beautiful eyes I'd ever seen. Dracon's couldn't hope to match. Here was the real thing. It was almost too absurd to comprehend. Why would the most powerful being in the Eight Realms want to be with me?

Suddenly, I felt ashamed of voicing my secret desire. I'd grown bolder since I arrived, but this was taking it too far. He'd already told me every reason this was a bad idea.

But he didn't look away.

My lips tingled with anticipation. Would he?

The breast of his damp suit rose and fell with heavier breaths, though his expression didn't change. "Don't say things you don't mean, Persephone. It's dangerous." His deep, cultured voice reverberated through my core.

"I mean it. I want to stay."

He took one predatory step forward. His power hit me like an aura, so palpable I stepped backward. Into my room. He followed.

I fought for breath. For a second, it felt like this was happening to somebody else, not me.

Those eyes were relentless, pinning me in place. "Why would someone like you want to stay here?"

At first, his question stung. *Someone like you.* Someone naïve and feminine, with a childlike love of color and flowers, someone whose strength didn't match the mighty beings here. But it did. I belonged here, as much as anyone else.

Or, did he want me to say the real reason aloud?

"I like it here," I said. "I like the people."

"The people." The words were a growl in his mouth. His pupils went wide.

I suddenly felt like he'd devour me. And I'd welcome it.

What did I have to lose? Embarrassment?

"You." My mouth dried but I held my ground.

"Be sure of what you say," he said, his voice gravel. "I told you I'm not a kind god."

"You are." I didn't give my reasons, but we both knew them.

"I'm rough, and violent..."

His tone sent another wet ache between my legs.

"And I won't go slow."

When I realized what he meant, my cheeks flamed.

Hades panted, clearly holding himself back. Heat from his body soaked into my front. We didn't touch, but I sensed every place he got close. His thigh almost touched mine. If I reached out my hand, I could take his.

"Yes... yes," I managed.

23

PERSEPHONE

Hades' hand compulsively flew to my hair, gripping it at the nape of my neck to crane me toward him. I moaned.

"You'll let me take you how I want? You'll let me take you till it hurts? Be sure." His final command sliced over me, brutal. He'd transformed into something feral. All his protests were burning in the wake of his overwhelming desire. For me.

In answer, I palmed his firm chest and clutched a fistful of his dripping shirt to draw him to me. He was all warm, hard muscle. He could take me however he wanted.

Our lips crashed together. His were demanding. He forced me open and lapped up my taste. My tongue met his, welcoming. It felt sinful to stand under Hades like this, mouth wide to take him in, but I wanted more, more. The scruff on his chin rasped against my face.

His calloused fingers lifted my skirt and ran roughly over my bare hip before he dragged the dress over my head.

I'd never been naked with a man. I expected it to feel

exciting and freeing, and it was, but my legs kept shifting to compensate for the discomfort of leaving myself exposed, open to inspection. My arms moved to cover my nipples, my slit. I didn't want to stop. I just was overwhelmed. He was so godlike and I was... new.

"Fuck," Hades breathed, taking me in.

A dark form ripped out of Hades' back. He grimaced in pain. "No!" he cried.

I glanced behind me. A mirror image of Hades, all black, with no distinct features but a perfect, solid outline, flew to meet me. Its breath blew in my face as it pressed itself fully against my back. I flinched at the contact.

The shadow didn't listen to Hades' protest, but it did seem to hear Hades' next command. "Don't hurt her!"

"Unless she wants it," came the rasping reply.

I could feel every muscle in its torso as it reached around to move my arms for better access to my breast. Palming the sensitive skin and not avoiding the nipple, the shadow took what he wanted. I squirmed under the new sensation.

A smirk spread over Hades' face. Relief. The shadow held me, groped me, made me gasp as he ground against my ass. Hades frantically removed his shoes, his jacket, his shirt, his pants. I stared in awe. He had massive shoulders and a chest I wanted to bite. Muscles rippled down the length of his cut torso to a deep V. His cock bounced up, hard and ready.

With a snarl, he was on me again, scooping up my ass to press me against him. "We'll take you right here," he grated against my ear, rubbing himself against me in barely contained, flexing motions.

We. I was crushed between two hard bodies, both panting

unevenly with lust. I drowned in the feel of their muscles undulating against me.

Then a spike of craving as Hades groped between my legs, grazing the spot where I needed friction. His fingers continued inside me, pushing deep. I squeezed my thighs together to cure the ache.

"No." The shadow gripped my neck, not hard but enough to tip my head back so I couldn't move. My hair flowed over its dark shoulder. "Open for us." I thought I saw a flash of teeth.

I obeyed, spreading my legs.

"Wider," hissed the shadow.

Hades' fingers dominated me, made me sopping. He crammed in one, two, three, pumping in and hooking inside.

I whimpered. It hurt, but I only wanted more.

Hades was brutally efficient when he removed his fingers and got to the task at hand, gripping himself and pushing inside. I winced at the pain. Even though I was slippery-slick, no one had ever been inside me. And now I was about to take two. I felt delirious.

"That's it." Hades bared his teeth and thrust hard. I was pushed back into the shadow, who held me upright with his big body.

"Oh gods," I moaned.

"Which one?" demanded the shadow, slapping me sharply on the hip.

"Hades, Hades!"

Hands were everywhere, touching me, squeezing me, and Hades kept up his merciless pace, sinking deeper with each thrust. Bodies writhed against me. He consumed me like a current. I never wanted to resurface. He was dark water and I wanted to drown.

He grunted as he filled me to the root, his balls swinging against me. I felt filthy and so, so good. He hooked me by the back of the knees and hauled me up to sit on his hips. My back grew colder without the shadow firm against me. Then I realized what they were doing.

Impaled on one side, I spread wide on the other to give the shadow entry. Nerves bubbled up. Would I be able to take two at once? Hades had to work to get inside me. Even now I felt full, his hard length jammed inside me as I flexed my walls around him.

Hands spread my ass and slapped it. The sharp pain made me even wetter.

"Do it again," Hades ordered.

The shadow obeyed, harder this time.

Again and again and again, until I was crying out. Hades bounced me on his cock and I was transported. There was only him inside me and around me, our sweaty bodies grinding together, and those glazed, piercing eyes drinking in my disheveled, pain-and-pleasure drunk face.

The stiff head of another cock pushed against my backside. There was no way it would fit.

"Take it," the shadow ordered, pressing harder. I strained, but couldn't do it.

"Fit him in," came Hades' deep voice. "Don't you want to bounce on both of us at once while we fuck you?"

"Yes," I groaned. And screamed, as the shadow stabbed in. Hardly anything separated the two hard cocks as they sawed into me on both sides.

I was frantic. Maybe I would pass out. All around me came the low straining noises of Hades taking his pleasure. He was uneven, each piece of him thrusting at its own pace with me mashed in the middle. Sweat dripped from Hades' hair onto my shoulder.

The shadow's hand wedged between us and found my clit. I swore, louder and louder. He swore too. The muscular arms holding me up flexed with exertion. Though I was bobbing, world spinning, I fell forward and sank my teeth into Hades' pectoral muscle like I lusted to do at the beginning.

"She likes to bite," said the shadow. He sounded excited. "What if I... bite that... pretty little neck?"

I don't know what noise I made. Relief? Excitement? Something well and truly lewd.

The shadow huffed, still rolling his hips against me. His hot breath cooled the sweat pooling in my throat. And teeth sank between my neck and shoulder. I cried out.

"Keep doing that," Hades demanded. "Not hard."

I wanted to protest—it felt so good I wanted him to bite hard—but then the shadow's tongue flicked out to lick me as he sucked. I couldn't speak. I could only feel. If Hades told the shadow not to bite me too hard, he had a reason.

"Fuck." Hades pulled at the back of my knees as if he could pull me closer, push himself even deeper. I ricocheted between Hades on one side and the vampire shadow on the other, movements growing more erratic.

We were close, all three of us. I could feel it. Hear it in the cries ripping from my throat as I ground against Hades' groin. Shudders of pleasure rebounded through my entire slick body.

Hands, chests, ass, legs. And two hard cocks inside me rubbing against each other.

My head fell back, legs spasming as my pussy contracted around him in waves. White light burst in my vision when the tension was too much. Release coursed through me. Hades and the shadow saw me through it, keeping the pace, holding me up. Then it was their turn. Nearly in tandem, they ground out curses and groans and shot their cum inside me.

Nearly unconscious, I flopped in their arms, eyes fluttering closed. I felt sore and weak and used. And utterly in heaven.

Hades adjusted me so I lay across his arms. Between my legs, I was raw and bleeding. I probably got some of those juices on him, but I also felt sure he didn't mind. I curled against his chest, my nipples still hard with arousal. But now I didn't care. I wanted him to feel them poke the firm skin of his side.

I didn't feel the shadow anymore.

Hades' stomach swelled against me with his breathing. It was calming, like being on the ocean.

"You're a brave girl," he murmured, breathless, kissing my forehead.

"That was wonderful."

"Mmm." The noise, hungry and amused, echoed through my chest in the most delicious way. "Then let's make that the warm up, Persephone."

"Seph."

"What?"

"Seph, please."

A dark chuckle. "Persephone, if you stay here, I'm your king and you do what I say."

My insides wriggled with pleasure.

Because that was the most staggeringly erotic thing that had ever happened to anyone. And it happened to me. And it just *might* happen again.

Hades would protect me. He'd proven it time and time again. I wanted to melt into his body and eat him for breakfast. Then, I wanted him to command me any way he wished.

24

HADES

I was fucked. There was no question.

As I lay beside Persephone, both of us still naked and damp from the rain and the sex, I knew I'd made a mistake.

And I didn't fucking care.

I found the Qa-a-ka word for beautiful—an incongruous mess of rasping sounds—and whispered it aloud, smoothing a strand of her dark hair behind her ear. She nestled into my chest. I wanted to take her inside me like I could the shadow.

Which she hadn't feared. Which had heightened her pleasure. I felt it in the way her slick pussy clenched compulsively around me. Thinking about it made me half-hard again. She liked the biting, the rough thrusting of two cocks inside her. She didn't fear my dark side like everyone else did. Now, I didn't believe it was because she was naïve. My innocent goddess had a dark side too.

A corner of my mouth lifted in a smirk. Such dirty desires

inside that sweet exterior. I pressed a lingering kiss to Persephone's temple. She sighed contentedly.

The post-coital haze was finally wearing off enough to think. I sat up. That—*that*—was her first time (fucking hell). I rose to fetch a cloth and a cup of water. Outside her warmth, the dark bedroom felt cold.

"Up," I said when I returned.

She murmured protests. I began cleaning her up with the cloth. There was more blood than I remembered.

Once I was done, I slipped my arm around her back and raised her myself, settling her on my lap. She opened her bright eyes. "Are you all right?" I asked seriously. "Did you enjoy all of that?" I was mad for most of it, so I couldn't be sure. All that blood...

"Oh," she groaned, the sound indecent. My chest clenched. "Yes, I did. If... you want to do it again...?"

I did, but I growled, pushing the cup of water into her hands. "Drink first."

She adjusted her position on my lap, accidentally tapping my lengthening cock, sending a shockwave through me. She winced as she sat up. When she caught me looking at her in a question, she explained, "Just sore. I'm fine." Her skin went dark and she dropped her eyes.

I chuckled. I had done that—marked her body with my own. With all of me. Something about sharing her with my other self had made the release even more explosive. I'd felt a hint of every shadow sensation as he speared her from the back. My gods, she was divine from every angle. I hid none of me, and she hid none of her.

I raised my chin at the cup in her hands. "Drink that. You need it."

She obeyed, taking a sip and then thirsty gulps.

Truth lurked in the silence. I couldn't stay. I had too much to do. But, damn it! All I wanted was to worship Persephone's body, to care for her, to teach her pleasure beyond her wildest imagination.

Her soft hip rested against my lower stomach. Every place we touched felt like a revelation. Hot and sweet and all-consuming, but, like a building orgasm, with the jerking sensation of imminent loss of control. My mind was trying to scream a warning, but Persephone was everywhere, filling all but the most remote thoughts.

I can't stay.

Centuries of telling myself, "No, don't fuck that person", "No, that's a bad idea", "No, I need to stay focused", "No, keep it professional" finally poked through into my consciousness. Reflex.

Persephone covered her breasts with her forearms while she drank, as if we hadn't just devoured each other. The juxtaposition flamed my skin.

I shifted so she could sit on the blankets and I could stand. "Thank you."

I met her eyes, tilted up to meet mine. Real affection lived there, not just the lust I'd seen blaze an hour ago. It hurt me, but it was good hurt. I smiled. "Persephone," I said, "when the two most dangerous beings in the world fuck you at once, you don't say thank you."

"What should I say?" Hope flared in her face. She clutched the cup to her collarbone. There was that juxtaposition again.

I reached for my discarded trousers lying next to the shock-ingly pink pool of her dress, considering. "When can I do it again?"

She beamed.

Yes, I was well and truly fucked.

THE SMART PART OF MY BRAIN HAD FRIED LIKE EGGS. Marzanna knew it too, judging by the way she looked at me.

"The spirits?" she prompted, after I'd gone idiotically silent.

I clasped my hands behind my back, rolling on the balls of my feet, trying anything to ground myself in this moment. There was the model of the Far Realm spreading over the floor of my office. There were the curtains. There was the map. There was Marzanna staring with red eyes in a white face.

"They have temporary lodging, don't they?" I asked.

"Yes, but soon they won't fit."

I grunted, looked at the model for the ten thousandth time. *What would Persephone think? She tethered them all here. What about that rocky plain?*

"I'll mull over the options I've narrowed down and let you know in the morning."

"Very good, my lord." A pause. "I thought you'd be more pleased by Seph's accomplishment at the dock. She seems to think you didn't care. Consider thanking her for taking such an enormous weight from your shoulders." Marzanna's words carried a bite that made my latent guilt surge. At least I could think of a few ways to thank Persephone now...

"I am pleased."

"You appear somewhat distracted, my lord."

"I'm fine."

Marzanna sighed, obviously annoyed on Persephone's behalf. "I've left the record of the last session's petitioners, and your language tutor left some papers for you as well."

"Mm."

"Do you require anything else?"

I *required* Persephone in my bed, even though I'd just left her an hour ago. But I said, "No." This thing between us was too fragile. If I looked at it straight on or told anyone else, the illusion would burst. And I'd burst with it.

I knew it was ridiculous to assume it could last.

I knew it was selfish of me to want Persephone—her strawberry scent and awesome powers of life. But that was just it. A god of the dead and a goddess of life...?

There I was, getting too close to the truth.

"You may go."

Marzanna inclined her antlered head and stepped out.

The spirits really did need a place to call their own. The issue that had scratched at the back of my mind had reached a crisis point. Besides my model on the floor and the map on the wall, I had a desk-sized version I could roll out and annotate. That was where I kept all records of ancient boundary lines, tribal territories, mine locations, and the like.

Many of the humans' lives had been difficult. The Far Realm wasn't a soft place, but if I chose the right area, they could have a soft afterlife, protected from the most fearsome monsters.

Where, where...?

More of my euphoria frittered away. As I'd feared, I couldn't focus at all. With every blink, I saw Persephone squeezed between us, lips parted, gleaming with sweat.

Bring her here. Release your frustrations.

My head swam. My shadow was wrong. Persephone deserved the best of me. Honestly, she deserved much better.

Let me get her for us.

No!

A petulant pause. *She likes what I do to her.*

I couldn't argue there. I had firsthand proof. When my other self had bitten her, she'd opened like a flower, soaking my dick buried deep inside her. Hell, she'd bitten *me.*

Leave her alone tonight, I finally told him. *Let her heal.*

A wicked smile stole over my face.

Another glance at the model of the kingdom made it dissipate like steam.

It was time to focus. If I could. Persephone stirred all my insides so thoroughly that I wasn't convinced I could ever focus on anything other than her again.

Maybe a different task. Something more concrete than searching for an elusive location to provide an afterlife to thousands of spirits.

I wandered back to my desk, running fingers back through my hair. The small pile of papers Marzanna had alluded to lay there.

Send shadow to border of Aridian forest and Northlands in two weeks, read one note.

That conversation felt like it had happened last month, not earlier today. Faintly, above me, rain still washed the windows, even this far north. The clouds had moved.

I flicked to the next sheet. A warding spell in Qa-a-ka, it looked like, though I could only read a couple of the words. Good. Even if I couldn't cast it to reinforce Abaddon, someone could. I sounded out the chant. It left my mouth dry.

A thick feeling, like sludge, crawled through me. I shouldn't have done it. I shouldn't have fucked Persephone.

After hundreds of years of carefully cultivated practice, you'd think I could keep my body in check. Her beauty pierced me in a way I didn't understand. It wasn't just visual, although that was a feast, with her bronze skin and light eyes, glossy black hair and eager curves. No. I couldn't find the words to describe it. It was like she saw a younger version of me, when I was wilder, still angry but zealous for the right thing. Less jaded. Before I'd sculpted my image thorn-sharp.

It wasn't hard to inspire fear once people saw what my other self could do. The gods wouldn't have won the Great War without me.

I was raw in front of Persephone. I didn't trust myself.

I snorted. *Rightly so.* Temptation called and I answered. It didn't matter that she trembled in my arms, her skin growing dewy and flushed. I knew I could elicit pleasure. And pain.

The heavy feeling grew. I still held the stack of papers loosely in my fingers. *Not now.* Instead, I paced.

Gods, I needed a drink. But my mind was fucked up enough already. I was trying to think clearly, not fall deeper under Persephone's spell. If I were better, maybe I could deserve her.

We're not better, the shadow chimed in.

No shit.

We're stronger and richer and more powerful. She wants darkness. Give her what she wants.

Something sour rested on the back of my tongue. Disgust at myself, at all the pieces of me that weren't worthy of Persephone's light and shouldn't have taken advantage of her. My stomach writhed. I couldn't remember wanting something as much as I wanted to be with Persephone. It was a fantasy, but the most purely seductive fantasy I could think of. I'd had the barest taste of what a life together could entail. Light and dark.

If I let her, she would *see* me. But I couldn't let that happen. The sight alone would rot the beautiful innocence and belief in others that gleamed in her eyes.

I stopped pacing.

First thing tomorrow, I'd call her here and give her the truth.

My body tensed as though preparing to battle all the evil of the god-prison. Was I strong enough to break this hope?

For her, for her, I chanted to myself. *Don't be a monster...*

The shadow sulked, dangerously upset. *Speak for yourself.*

❧ 25 ❧

PERSEPHONE

I woke alone, sore and stretched out. Half-finished water sat beside the bed. Edges of the blanket tucked around my nude body.

I buried my face in the pillow, smothering a grin. I still couldn't believe it. What a day yesterday had been, and today would be even better.

In the morning, I'd used my power to rescue all the untethered spirits at once.

In the evening, Hades and I...

I could still hardly think it to myself. He wanted me, and it wasn't just because I was more powerful than either of us guessed. Hades was a wave, drowning me. He saw me naked. He *touched* me naked.

I glanced at the books I'd requested from Marzanna. This was better than Dracon and Esmeralda, because it was real. I'd *really* run my hands and teeth over Hades' broad, muscular chest. The most feared god among the deathless had come undone in my arms as he pumped inside me. The memory made me wet again.

Time to get up.

I'd see Hades again soon—hopefully very soon—but now I needed to tend to the spirits, check if the power still held overnight. Best not to soil the blankets anymore too.

A smile played on my lips as I moved my pink dress to the side and selected one of the other choices hanging on a rack in a corner of the room. Lavender this time, short-sleeved but long and trimmed with fur. It was still chilly. I thought my memories might warm me up, but they only made my skin more sensitive. I shivered pleasurably in the cool air. Even smells were sharper—ash from the fireplace, rain from the deluge last night, and that deep, minty scent that accompanied Hades wherever he went.

Before going down to the dock, I would figure out where the spirits were staying in the fortress and consult with them. The humans ought to have some say in what they wanted their afterlife to look like. What would be peaceful for them? Was there anything a deathless god would overlook that Hades could provide?

It was like we were a team already.

You're rushing things. My cheeks heated. Yes, I'd been very rushed last night. Maybe Hades didn't feel as excited as I did. He wasn't a god with a reputation for affairs—the opposite, actually, which gave me a surge of pride—but other information about the Far Realm had been wrong too.

Did he see me only as a distraction, like he'd said in the greenhouse?

The thought made me still. I didn't like it. I didn't have

much experience, or any, before last night, but I understood Hades well enough. Didn't I?

He was proud and professional, elegant and severe. He liked his world orderly, didn't allow himself the luxury of feelings very often, but cared deeply, self-sacrificially, for the citizens of his kingdom.

Though, I thought, he could have done better with the human corpses coming in. Probably, he didn't have enough helpers to change the system that just piled up bodies. I added that to my list of things to consider. I was a goddess now —*really* a goddess—and not just a laborer at the dock. My opinion would mean something to him. There had to be a better way to deliver the humans to shore and then to their afterlife. When I saw him next, I'd ask him lots of questions. After he and his vampire shadow had their way with me.

That shadow. It didn't scare me like it had next to the prison wall, but reckless danger emanated from every curl of smoke, from every black line. It was Hades, but with pointed teeth and pointed nails. The demon inside. It gave me what I was too afraid to ask for, because maybe it was wrong to want so much force. Some of the sensations I'd dreamed about, though, had been the shadow's scraping nails across my breasts and his teeth sinking into my neck.

I touched the spot under my jaw. It was still tender. The reflective window revealed a dark mark there. I finger combed my hair, satisfied with my reflection, and went out.

I hadn't forgotten about the manticore but I'd wrestled with more dangerous beings now. Anxiety didn't coat my heart.

"Marzanna!" I called quietly down the bare stone corridor. My voice echoed off the vaulted ceiling. She would know where the spirits were. It was early, but she never seemed to sleep anyway. "Mar—!"

A black figure flashed in my vision. Then everything went black. My lungs seized in surprise.

Then, light.

I blinked, confused. Hades stood in front of me, dressed in a dark gray suit, long legs crossed at the ankle as he leaned back against a massive desk. Muscles in his crossed arms filled out the sleeves of his jacket. Those piercing gray eyes sliced me like metal, but his expression was neutral.

I would have smiled except for the defensive body language. Was I in trouble? My old patterns of thinking couldn't help creeping back.

To my left stalked the shadow, openly staring at me. The strong, Hades-like shape moved like a panther, so dark he almost looked like a void in the room. He'd brought me to Hades again.

Hades' gaze flicked to it, then back at me. He uncrossed his arms, gripping the edge of the desk behind him instead. "Persephone," he said softly. Was that regret in his voice?

I stiffened. "Is everything all right? Has something happened?"

"No, no. A lot has happened, but nothing bad since last night." A flare of the lust I'd seen last night. A tightening of fingers against the wood. "I returned to the docks a couple hours ago, and your power still holds."

I smiled, then drew up short. "A couple hours ago?"

"I don't need much sleep."

"I was going to do that this morning. You didn't have to—"

"It's my kingdom. I need to know what goes on. And it's

still working. Spirits are returning as soon as they reach that spot. It's... miraculous. You've done amazing work."

His compliment, so low and hoarse it lifted the hairs on my arms, was sweeter because he rarely gave them.

Maybe we were okay. For a minute I'd thought he regretted his decision to be with me.

"Thank you," I said.

He smirked, there then gone. I mirrored the expression as I remembered when I'd said that for a different reason.

"I want to keep helping them—find them a permanent place, improve procedures at the docks... The ones I met yesterday are so amazing. There was this girl and her brother who went through so much and when they found each other..." Emotion clogged my throat.

Hades regarded me with a new expression, with his brow slightly furrowed, head cocked to the side. The rest of his features relaxed. He dropped his eyes.

"Something is wrong," I pressed. "If you don't want to tell me, that's okay. But... I'm here for you." It felt foolish to say that to someone so powerful.

At my words, his eyebrows lifted, though he didn't lift his eyes for another moment. Gathering a breath, he locked his gaze on mine again. A bolt shot through me at the connection.

Tentatively, I took a small step forward. Hades hadn't moved from his desk which he gripped like an anchor. My heart thudded with apprehension I couldn't name.

"Persephone, I appreciate everything you've done here with the spirits and with me, but your job here is done. You don't need to invent more tasks for yourself. I know you don't enjoy living in the Far Realm, so you may return to Kantharos. If you have any input to share about the spirits before you leave, I'd like to hear it before you go."

I stood like a stone. Cold enveloped me despite the fur-lined dress. "You still want me to leave?"

"I thought you'd be pleased."

My pulse kicked up. "Pleased? I don't want to leave now."

"If you need a couple days—"

"I don't want to leave." A sob caught in my throat, but I caught it in time, just like the human spirits. "I didn't want to leave."

Was that why he chose to have sex with me last night, right after I'd finished the job he needed from me? Because he knew I'd be going away?

My breathing was irregular. "Why are you pushing me out?"

"I'm not pushing you out," he declared with a hint of irritation. "I'm trying to do the right thing."

At some point, the shadow had disappeared. Gone back into him or whatever it did, probably. For some reason, that left me feeling even more alone.

I balled my hands into fists. "I thought..." But I wasn't sure how to go on. It felt absurd to say I thought he'd called me in here—to his office, I guessed—to repeat what we had done last night. I tried something else. "I would rather stay here with you." The last two words felt risky, but I was bolder now. Actually, the whole thing felt risky. When had I started to think this way? I'd been desperate to get out before. Now, I had no desire to return to the gardens, except as a visitor. Here was where I belonged.

"That isn't a good idea." He dropped the sentence like he

were in a business meeting. Smooth. Detached. Totally in charge.

I pushed through the awkwardness. "It's my life. I'm a grown goddess and can make my own decisions. If you'd rather not be with me..."

"That's not it," he snapped, his fingers finally prying away from the desk's edge. "I shouldn't have done what I did with you. It was unprofessional and, I'm sure, gave you the wrong impression."

I felt as if I'd been struck. "Wrong impression?" I drew in a breath, cheeks burning. "You wanted that. I felt it. I know it was my first time, but... you wanted that."

"Persephone." The way he sighed my name warmed my insides like stew. "That's more reason for you to go home. Show the people there what you can do. If the power ever stops at the wharf, I'll call for you."

"I don't want to go home. I can do more here. You always thought I could do more."

"I know you can. That mother of yours kept you doing little flower petal tricks for too long. She had no idea her daughter was one of the most powerful goddesses I've ever seen." Something hitched in his face, as if he'd said too much.

"See?" I said, taking another step forward. "I belong here."

"Persephone." This time a growl, a warning.

"Don't cut me off." I felt reckless, and wouldn't simply bow to Hades' suggestion. It was as if the girl Persephone had dissolved yesterday and a new Persephone spoke now. "Why do you want me to leave? At least be honest with me."

The entire room darkened and stretched, though I couldn't point out where. Large maps distorted behind him. Bookcases wavered as if they were underwater. In front of me, Hades blazed like dark fire.

"I am carnage. I am death." I didn't even see his lips move.

The office shrank back into itself. Silence sucked in where the grating words had boomed a second before.

Hades observed me, carefully cold.

My arms trembled. Fear clenched my heart, but it felt more like adrenaline than terror. I knew Hades was dangerous. And a secret part of me loved that.

"I know," I said. I didn't move from where I stood rooted in the center of the floor.

"I don't think you do."

"You're also the one who tucked me in last night."

He looked away, offering a view of his profile and jawline.

"I think you're kind too," I persisted. "Deep down, where it matters."

He scoffed.

"Even if... yesterday... you don't want more of that," I said, "I want to stay here to help you with the spirits." Another step forward. "What do *you* want?"

His throat worked before he turned back to me. Beautiful. He was beautiful in a savage, cultured way I craved.

"What I shouldn't," he finally answered, eyes boring into me so intensely that I knew just what he meant.

"I want that too," I whispered.

He gripped the desk edge again. "I'm no good for you, Persephone. You... Fuck, you deserve your own realm, not a god unleashing all his dark fantasies on you."

My body all but turned inside out. *All his dark fantasies.*

"I am not good," he repeated, emphasizing each word.

"We've killed thousands, and it wasn't always right. I'm obsessive and violent. You are kind and beautiful and determined and so fucking powerful I wonder where my power falls in comparison, because I bet there's more. You can do more good than me, so don't let me keep you here. Please."

Please. Had he ever used that word with me? His language was commands, not requests.

I closed the gap between us. "You're not keeping me here anymore. I'm choosing to stay. This is where I belong." His vulnerable declaration made me surer than ever.

We breathed in the air between us. His posture relaxed a little and I was leaning toward him. Our foreheads touched.

"You are more than the darkness," I whispered so quietly he might not have heard me. Just felt the warm breath on his lips. "But I like that part too."

His forehead scrunched under mine. He closed his eyes.

Inhale. Exhale.

"Then bend over the desk."

❦ 26 ❦

HADES

ore than the darkness.

Persephone didn't run when I laid out the reasons she should flee. She just gazed back at me, earnest and resolute. She didn't know everything—Divine, I doubted *I* could list all my sins—but she knew enough.

She wanted me, darkness and all. Not just my body, which people had lusted after before. Not just for a favor or mercy. Darkness. And. All.

So I'd give her some darkness.

Following my order, Persephone obediently moved past me and bent over the desk in my office. She liked when I took control. The knowledge hardened my already stiff cock.

I smacked her rear end. "Arms above your head. Stretch them."

She reached out right as my frenzied other self broke free again. The shadow and I looked at each other. I never had to explain.

Tossing the pale purple dress up over her hips, I left the

shadow to do his work, getting a delectable look at her plump ass first. Before, I'd had ghost memories of seeing it, but now I had my own. I headed around to the other side of the desk.

A crack sounded. Persephone squeaked. The shadow caressed the spot he'd spanked. And again. "She likes it," he growled, breathless. Another spank and he reached underneath to feel how slick she was. My own fingers ghosted wet.

I crouched in front of Persephone's face so I could look her in the eyes, which were liquid-dark with desire. I shrugged off my jacket, flicked open the buttons of my shirt.

"Grab my shoulders." She did.

She flinched as the shadow hit her again, but then her mouth went slack. My own heartbeat kicked up. *My gods.*

"What does she taste like?" muttered my other self, looming dark above her. He squeezed her hip hard before kneeling and biting into the meat of her thigh.

I inspected Persephone's face. Just erotic pleasure. No protests to stop.

The phantom feeling of her inner thigh in my mouth drove me mad. The tastes rose higher. The underside of her round butt.

"You'll take both of us again," I rasped.

"Yes," she breathed.

"Beg for it."

"I want..."

I pulled back to stretch her shoulders further. "Beg with your body."

Her grip on me tightened. She widened her legs.

"Your mouth," I said, squeezing her cheeks so those

luscious lips would open further. "He'll fuck you and you'll fuck me with your mouth. Beg."

She only made a noise, but it was a noise I knew I'd hear every night in my dreams.

The shadow smacked her again.

"You want it?" I goaded.

We were all mad, barely on the brink. Another test of my dark sexual tastes and she ate them up like strawberries.

I grunted as I stood and freed my straining dick from my pants.

The shadow shoved himself in her pussy. She bobbed toward me with the force of his thrusts. Hair fell haphazardly in her face.

"No, no," sang the shadow, grabbing a handful of her hair and pressing her forward toward me, head up.

I slid the sensitive head into her warm mouth. The shadow's rhythm was her rhythm was my rhythm. Her hands rose up to grasp my hips. Even when bursts of choking air feathered my steel cock, she didn't pull away or plead or try to speak. The shadow was relentless, jackknifing back and forth, punishing and needy.

"Oh fuck!" I stabilized myself flat-palmed on the table. "Persephone, suck harder."

She obeyed.

My abdominal muscles not so much clenched as spasmed. "Oh gods! Fuck!"

The desk groaned as it slid toward me.

The shadow's panting turned to animal growls. His bladed fingers grew longer. His hand came down on her ass.

A gurgling cry and full-body shudder as she came. I pulled

out to let her ride the orgasm. Despite being the godsdamn sexiest thing I'd ever laid eyes on, she was new. Maybe she didn't want a jet of hot cum down her throat. I glanced at her sweat-stained face, hair fallen back over it. She would like hot cum down her throat. Hell, she'd like two cocks in her mouth at once, I'd bet. Too late now. Next time.

I pumped myself—the matter of a second to get myself there, with Persephone laid out on my desk like that. The shadow came moments later, pounding jerkily into her a few more times before giving her one last hard spanking that brought water to her eyes.

Darkness and all.

Mistake or not, I'd stop pushing her away, since she made it clear she wanted to stay, even if that meant staying with me. Fear tugged lightly at my insides. But Persephone didn't look afraid.

Well, right now she looked like a goddess who'd been treated like a naughty, naughty girl. Her eyes were still closed.

I tucked myself back into my trousers and buttoned them, straightening my suit. My other self absorbed into me again, momentarily satisfied. Then I touched Persephone's arm lightly.

"Let's get you up."

Sleepily, she cracked open her eyelids and eased upright, flinching a little, but smiling too.

"You're mad, you know," I said, circling the desk again. Gods, she was beautiful, all mussed and soft from my rough attention. I could spend all day like this.

"Maybe," she conceded. "But I like it here."

"Here in the Far Realm, or my office, or..." I planted a kiss on her lips, not like our other hungry, desperate ones. This one was painfully sweet. My violence followed by her earnest tenderness. The thickness in my throat surprised me.

She stood—I partially held her up—and wrapped her arms around my neck.

"All of it," she said when she broke away. A coy smile curved her lips before dimming with embarrassment. She hid her face in my chest. I stroked her hair, relaxed and warm with her body against mine.

Suddenly, she straightened, turned her eyes on me. Blue as a winter sky above a dangerous sea. "I have a shift at the docks."

"Not right now." I took her hand and led her to the model of the Far Realm that took up an enormous portion of the floor. "Today, you're with me. If you're going to stay, I want you to help create a home region for the spirits." I swept my free hand above the model. "You can do that better here."

She pursed her mouth in a smile. "I'd like that."

"Can you use your ability anywhere?" I tried to keep my tone business-like and even, as it always was.

Usually was.

Persephone's nearness and my orgasm of a second ago made it difficult to say anything relevant to business. But she was right. There were always tasks to complete. I could manage to talk about one that concerned her, though it was difficult to care.

"I think so," she answered. "Do you mean the plants or tethering the spirits?"

"Both."

"I know I can grow plants anywhere. It's even easier since I did that thing at the docks. There's that grass in your room."

"Yes." That patch of grass and flowers that I kept alive ever since Persephone had showed off skills worthy of a goddess. She allured me then, but it was nothing compared to the glint that sparked like fire between us now every time we locked eyes. "That will be helpful if I choose that barren patch where you met the sirens." I pointed on the three-dimensional map at our feet.

She leaned to get a better look. "Why not there?" she countered, indicating a larger area.

"Part of that is cordoned off for spirits already, but the borders are dominated by feuding tribes of demi-gods who get nasty when anyone steps foot on their land. It's already at capacity."

"What about buildings with multiple stories? You could fit more in comfortably, then."

I squeezed her hand. It was a good idea. Why hadn't I thought of that? "Interesting. I'll consider it."

From the corner of my eye, I spotted some of the papers Marzanna had delivered earlier. The Qua-a-ka incantation. It could wait.

I took Persephone's hips and turned her to face me.

"That's not all we're doing," she laughed, incredulous. She must have seen in my expression that I had no patience for work.

"I'm curious about your mind. Such power, such good ideas, such dirty desires..." I chanted, low.

She took a deep breath under my hands, face turning hopeful.

Before I could focus on anything else, I had to make her feel like a queen. Maybe it was to make myself feel like less of a monster, or maybe it was to thank her for being the fucking incredible person she was. I didn't know and I didn't care. What I did know was my pants already tightening again. I was ready for another round.

"How are you feeling?" I asked, eyes dropping so she knew exactly what I was asking.

"It'll hurt, but that's fine," she answered quickly.

My dirty girl. I smirked, whisking us to my suite. We landed on the black silk sheets of the round bed. A half-moon headboard skimmed the wall, also black and carved with black roses. The skulls were real and had just been inlaid and painted to look like the rest. I never pretended to be anything but the god of death.

You stand down this time, I ordered the shadow. *This time, it's just me.*

A low growl of irritated submission. Honestly, I was surprised it was that easy.

"Now," I said to Persephone with a cold air of command, "take off your clothes and hold onto the headboard."

With the shadow out of the way, I could have her all to myself. Her eyes shone with anticipation as she obeyed. Insatiable. Just like me. The faint alarm bells calling *Don't trust it!* got quieter and quieter. And I drowned them out with her ecstatic screams.

❧ 27 ❧

PERSEPHONE

By the time Hades was finished with me, the curved headboard grew lush with greenery. In one swift motion, he detached my gripping hands and flipped me around. I landed soft on the bed, the springy turf teasing the top of my head.

There was something unguarded about his small, crooked smile as he looked down at me. I'd seen him stoic, angry, commanding, smug. I'd never seen him really... happy. He looked happy.

He smoothed the rough pad of his thumb under my eye.

I hadn't realized I'd been crying. His punishing thrusts and orders and rough touches hurt, but in the most delicious way. I wanted him to take his pleasure however he wanted. If I had let myself daydream about someone doing this to *me*, maybe I would have understood what kind of sex I'd enjoy.

Even now, the idea that Hades wanted me seemed crazy, like a dream I'd wake up from. Tomorrow, I'd find myself in Mother's modest house, smell loaves baking. It would be comfortable, I'd grab my book, work in the royal garden, and pine for a lover whose darkness spoke to something deep in my core.

I'd never be the same after this.

I wanted Hades.

And he wanted me.

"You've ruined my bed," he said, little more than a rumble. His smile stretched. I barely caught it.

My heartbeat's gallop calmed enough for me to talk. Not easily, though. Naked Hades lay on top of me. His hard muscles met my skin at a million points. He had that tousled hair I liked.

"Do you want me to ruin the rest of it?" I spread my hand against the blanket.

"I think you've done enough. Gods..." he breathed, and kissed me. "I keep thinking you'll realize what's happening and hate me."

I frowned. His gray eyes flashed under hooded lids. He meant it.

"Why would I hate you?"

He swiped a rogue tear from my other eye. "I haven't been easy on you."

My skin felt raw but I liked the burn. It meant Hades had been there and enjoyed it. I'd made the cold god of the dead ignite.

I drew a hand down his firm pectoral muscles. He shivered and I grinned.

"Have partners hated you before?"

"I don't have partners," came his clipped answer. He drew

in a deep breath that pressed on my belly. "Not for a long time. Until..." He hesitated, then met my eyes.

I willed him to continue.

He kissed my lips, hot and soft, before uttering a groan and sitting up. He balanced his elbow on one knee drawn up. Even naked and sweat-streaked, he was the picture of elegance.

I sat next to him, leaning against the cool green headboard. His black silk sheets gave the illusion that we sat on enchanted water.

"I didn't want to chain anyone here," he began, only a hint of the hoarseness he got in the heat of arousal. Now he was cultured again. "Poor choice of words." He cast me a roguish look.

I bit my lower lip to stop my smile.

"I mean, there have been a thousand reasons. Ask anyone in the Eight Realms. They don't want to spend the rest of their days here. Bad, they'll say. Terrifying. Good." He looked away a moment. His thoughts evidently went to distant pain, and I saw the sheer *ruler* in him. He'd seen unspeakable things. He'd probably done some too. That violent depth didn't scare me, though. It gave him power and gravity. He was an ancient force that stayed forever young, and he'd chosen me, made sure I didn't hurt too much after he plunged ruthlessly inside me.

"It's not just terrifying, though," I said.

"You met Drakaina." He popped up his eyebrows, half teasing. "But the thing I wanted most to avoid..." He went distant again as his lips formed words. "Was me."

I wanted to snuggle up against him, but this seemed hard for him to say, so I just listened, swirling one finger in a circle against the sheets.

"Once, I told you I was the most dangerous creature here," he said. "I wasn't exaggerating."

A chill ran down my back at the certainty in his voice. His face, also, burned with conviction.

"But I will try, with everything in my power, to give you whatever is good in me."

New tears replaced my old ones. I sniffed them back. Now I couldn't resist crawling closer and letting him wrap a solid arm around me. He set his chin on top of my head. "You have a lot of good," I said. That reminded me. I scanned corners of the big room. "Where's...?"

"He doesn't fall into my 'good' category," Hades answered gruffly, catching my meaning.

"Well..."

He gave a dark chuckle against my back. "My dirty girl, was one not enough for you?"

"One was perfect," I said, craning to look at him.

"It'll be hard to keep him away. And by hard I mean fucking impossible most of the time."

"I like that too."

He fell quiet, caressing the top of my thigh. "I've given him too long a leash with you. He's... unpredictable, Persephone."

"He's you," I murmured, picking up his hand and kissing the back of it.

We'd had this argument before, but I felt his response. The fear he had about his own darkness or maybe his inability to keep himself in check.

I had darkness and understood what it felt like to lack control. It was frightening and frustrating, but not enough for me to truly fear Hades. His power could crush and consume, but I got his protection. He could even be a little sweet. When he wasn't squeezing my throat and driving into me from behind. I flushed.

"He is behaving right now," Hades muttered, obviously still skeptical.

"Yes," I agreed. "He's you, and you wouldn't hurt me."

"Unless you want me to," he said, echoing the shadow's words from that first time.

My breath shallowed. "Exactly."

He drew a finger down the tender part at the front of my neck. "I don't understand how someone can be the sweetest fucking person I've ever met and still have the filthiest cravings."

I put my chin down, embarrassed and proud at once. I was still getting used to all of this—my power, being with Hades, everything. I didn't need to make myself smaller and easier to tame anymore. I could be as big as I wanted. Sometimes that felt like vertigo.

"I'm trusting you, too," Hades said, quieter, "when you say you want to stay."

I spun around and rose on my knees to face him. Curses surfaced in my mind. He was so beautiful. The hint of vulnerable uncertainty offered a new, tantalizing view. I took his strong face in my hands. The dusting of dark hair on his cheeks scratched my palms. "I do."

His features softened. "Clearly, you're insane."

We smiled at each other.

A knock sounded at the door.

Hades' face fell with annoyance. He didn't grab his clothes or even a blanket as he stalked away from the bed.

I pulled the sheet over my front, watching his firm butt as he went. I couldn't help it. It was an unfairly gorgeous butt.

The door was in the other room, where the shadow had thrown me down what felt like a lifetime ago. Although a huge archway connected the rooms, I couldn't see the visitor, only hear.

"...is here for your lesson," said a voice. Slightly familiar. It might have been the vampire I'd seen at the front door of the palace. It was hard to tell for sure, since an edge of unease raised the messenger's voice.

Marzanna usually worked part of my shift with me in the mornings, so that was why this was a different messenger. My skin tightened with the feeling I was doing something wrong, and not in a fun way. Wasn't I supposed to be helping with the Far Realm's monumental tasks?

"Cancel it," Hades replied. "Send him away with payment."

"A medium from the northlands offered a new protective spell for the prison." It sounded like the vampire was reading off a list, not facing down a naked, grumpy god.

"I'll need to see it first. Next week."

"And Demeter is here from Kantharos."

❦ 28 ❦

PERSEPHONE

I leapt out of bed, yanking the lavender dress over my head. My skin webbed with panicky static.

Demeter? Mother? Here, in the Far Realm? How had she even managed to cross the Stygian Sea?

My heart ricocheted wildly. I hadn't seen her in a long time. I missed her, but I didn't want to go back. I'd found a new life here. Maybe even a new love.

I hesitated before leaving Hades' bedchamber. Hades himself was stark naked at the door, hearing news from the messenger. If I walked up behind him, it wouldn't be difficult to figure out what we'd been doing. And doing and doing, all morning. Did he want other people to know?

"Demeter," Hades snapped, just out of eyeshot. "Where?"

"The goddess is in the receiving hall at the fortress," came the vampire's voice, holding steady.

"Did she say why?"

"She... requested to speak with you, Lord Hades."

The messenger was being diplomatic. My mother was kind

and warm and protective, but she was fierce too. I'd technically been kidnapped. Guilt twisted my stomach that I hadn't worried more about her state of mind. She must have been frantic after Hades stole me away.

She hadn't *requested* to see Hades. If I knew her, she demanded it.

"Tell her to wait. I'll meet her there." Hades' voice was too carefully controlled. Tense.

"As you wish, Lord Hades."

"Tell me that's all your news."

"Everything of immediate importance."

"Then go."

The heavy door fell closed. I emerged from the bedroom, passing between the obsidian pillars. Hades hadn't turned around. He stood with his head slightly bent. Then, he straightened, pivoted on his heel, and prowled back to the bedroom, passing me on the way.

"I'm sure you heard everything," he said, without looking at me.

"Mother's here," I breathed, watching Hades produce a jet-black suit and begin dressing.

"Do you want to come with me? This meeting will concern you." For an invitation, the words sounded impersonal. Something about him had disconnected.

"Of course. I need to see her."

At that, he finally looked at me. "Do you?" he snapped. Then, "I'm sorry. I... We'll go together." He fastened his fitted trousers and approached me. His bare chest, with its sinful trail of dark hair, made me warm again. He inhaled deeply. "The decision is always yours, if you want to stay or go."

When I started to protest, he cupped my cheek. "Darkness is alluring for a time, until you truly understand it. I won't be angry if you choose another way. I just ask that you return occasionally, since your help has been invaluable. The Far Realm needs the life in these fingers." He threaded our hands together.

"I told you what I wanted, and I stick to my word," I said.

"I won't be angry," he repeated in my ear, barely a whisper. "Even the God-King feared me in the end."

My breath stuck in my throat as he walked away.

❦ 29 ❧

HADES

Breathe in. Breathe out. Breathe in. Breathe out. And you, stay quiet.

A feral growl. *But she's ours!*

I greatly regretted letting my guard down. My other self was getting too used to freedom and was getting used to being out of control. I tightened the leash inside, but the darkness thrashed and whined. I was half afraid he would tear through me.

Demeter is her mother. They have a right to talk.

Or to leave.

Yes, I bit out. *Or to leave. Persephone can make her own choices.* I'd known since the beginning that it was in her best interest for her to leave, but damn if I didn't want her here, always, growing plants in wild places, warm and eager in my bed...

No, she stays.

You—I stopped walking to concentrate—*don't make a move. Don't make a sound. Let me handle this.*

Persephone's hand found mine. She could sense something

was wrong. Of course she could. It was written all over those blue eyes, so striking in her tan face.

"I'm fine," I said, and kept walking.

We'd walked through the air into the fortress, approximately where I'd arrived with Persephone the first time. Tall ceilings. Lots of nice blocks of stone. Nothing to impress Demeter, not that I cared if she was impressed.

The closer we got to the end of the hall, Persephone gently disentangled her hand from mine.

My muscles clenched in my effort to hold back the beast inside. I wouldn't be a possessive asshole if I could help it. All right, fine, I was a possessive asshole, but didn't want to show it.

I hated Demeter for having a legitimate claim on Persephone's affection. That wasn't fair of me, but life was never fair. If it were, I wouldn't have fucked Persephone.

A figure stood at the end of the hallway. Imperious. Not quailing before me.

I grabbed Persephone's hand again and gripped her fingers hard. My other self, for all its pacing and growling, preened at Demeter seeing me with Persephone.

She broke away.

"Mother!" She embraced Demeter, who glared murderously at me over her daughter's shoulder. I gazed coolly back.

Rip her to shreds. No one defies you like that!

I said stand down.

"Demeter," I said smoothly, linking my hands behind my back.

"Hades." No *Lord Hades* today. Judging from Demeter's red-faced anger, I was almost surprised to be addressed at all. The small, rational part of me knew I'd be relentlessly furious too if someone kidnapped Persephone from me.

Persephone let her mother go. "It's so good to see you," Persephone said in a rush, almost with embarrassment.

Demeter's hard gaze shifted from me to her daughter, and she gasped. "What's this? Seph, what are all these bruises?" Her fingers lightly traced the marks I'd made on Persephone's neck and arms.

"Nothing." Persephone folded in on herself, blushing deeply. Every movement, making herself smaller, though her power outstripped her mother's like the sun outstripped the light of the stars.

"It's not nothing. Did he hurt you?" Demeter asked quietly.

"Did you come here for a particular purpose?" I cut in. "Persephone is capable of making her own choices. My need here was great enough that I required her services. Once it was possible for her to leave, the decision was hers. You did not need to come at all."

"This, from the god who stole my daughter!" she spat. Caressing Persephone's face, she went on. "I would have done anything to get her back. I don't care about your problems here, *my lord*. She belongs with me."

"Bold words to hurl at the god of the dead." My words slowed from the effort of keeping my other self at bay. Each word out of Demeter's mouth made the shadow more feral.

"I'm fine, Mother," Persephone said, putting a tiny bit of distance between them. "The work here is important, and Hades has taken care of me."

"You don't need to say that," Demeter replied, obviously referencing the bruises.

I flattened my mouth, but Persephone had found her voice, so I let her explain.

"I'm not just saying that," she said. "He brought me here to help reunite human spirits with their bodies so they can have an afterlife. It's hard, but I can have anything if I ask, if I'm off-duty."

Demeter gave a rueful chuckle. "Seph, your ability is beautiful. Healing flowers makes the world a more wonderful place. The royal gardens don't look as vibrant without you there to work your magic. But you can't save dead humans. He's asking too much of you. And besides, even if you could, why would you? They can find peace in the ether, not in this place."

I couldn't hold back any longer. "I assure you, I chose well. I knew she had enough skill." I couldn't keep the dangerous edge out of my voice.

"You stay away from my daughter! I know full well why you took her away, and it wasn't for some imagined help for the humans."

"I have helped them," Persephone said, louder now. She frowned at her mother.

That's my girl. Tell her.

"I saved tons of spirits from disappearing. They're staying here, even." Her head swiveled, but the wing where the spirits temporarily stayed was far out of sight.

"You couldn't have, darling. Seph, I believe in you more than anybody and love you more than anybody, but I know you. You would defend anyone simply because you're a kind person. You don't have to defend him."

Persephone took another step back. "I'm not lying. Hades helped me believe in my own power." Tears suddenly welled in her eyes. "I can really help people here, Mother. I like it more than the royal gardens."

Demeter bent close to her ear. "Gods will say anything to—"

"Persephone has saved hundreds of souls from nothingness," I cut in. "She brings life wherever she goes. The least you can do is be happy for her."

"How can I be happy if you're feeding her lies to tempt her to your bed?"

"Mother!" Persephone covered her mouth.

I stalked forward, unable to hold myself back anymore. "Your daughter is not a stupid child. She is a powerful goddess who can change the world."

"Don't act like you know her better than I do," Demeter snarled.

"Apparently, I know the important things. And I learn more every day."

"So you admit you want her?"

"Gladly."

Persephone's mouth fell open. Intensity shot through her gaze as she looked first at me, then at her mother. Maybe I'd gone too far, but I wasn't known for kindness.

"Seph, you're coming home." Demeter grabbed Persephone's arm. Her finger touched one of the bruises I'd put there. Persephone's skin indented under the controlling grip.

The shadow tore free.

❊ 30 ❊

PERSEPHONE

Darkness.

That was all I saw.

One second, my mother with a frenzied look in her eyes.

The next, a shrieking mass of darkness. Or maybe the shriek was Hades. That horrible sound was storm and weather but it was masculine, desperate.

I screamed and raised my arm—the one Mother didn't squeeze tightly—to shield my eyes. What was going on? Dread filled me, like prey before a predator, but I couldn't see anything. Couldn't feel—

A force ripped me away from Mother, into the dense cloud of black.

"Mine," I heard, a subterranean growl that could have come from inside myself.

Then I understood.

The darkness materialized into a person who held me tight

around the waist, but kept scrabbling to keep me closer. Long-nailed hands dragged at my clothes. I gasped at shocks of knife-like pain. The body became like iron. Immovable. Unbeatable.

Grimacing against discomfort, I tried to twist around, to see Hades' shadow. "I'm staying here," I pleaded. "Please don't hurt her."

The shadow bared its pointed teeth. Something dripped from them onto my shoulder before he pushed me behind him. He stood between me and my mother.

Mother was a goddess herself, strong in every situation I'd ever seen her. But even she looked afraid. She stood up straight and looked it in the eye, but her skin had gone sickly pale and trembled all over.

"Don't hurt her," I repeated.

A snarl was my only answer. Tears prickled at my eyes again.

The shadow stretched out his arm, like an animal playing with its meal. Mother took in shaky breaths, wincing from its touch. Her bravery moved me.

"GO!" roared a voice. Hades' voice.

I whirled around. He looked elemental in his rage. His gray eyes glowed, his face had somehow become gaunt.

"Never come back here. You'll never go near Persephone or her mother again so long as I live."

The shadow creature slowly turned, spine curling like a frightened cat's. There was something tentative about the way it looked at Hades. Almost as if he couldn't take him seriously. For a second, I felt pity for him. It was bad, but it was Hades. Had anyone ever cared for it?

"Go!" Hades shouted again, wild-eyed with fury.

The shadow, with all its manifest darkness, wailed away into the night.

I released a breath, adrenaline swirling down. In the sudden emptiness, up my arm roared pain. Pain. Splintering, muscle-deep shards of burning ice. I whimpered and held the throbbing arm with my other hand. When I moved, my stomach ached too. The shadow had injured me. Badly.

"Darling!" Mother cried, meeting me as I stumbled to my knees. She looked me in the eye. Her own were huge with worry. "Seph, I can't believe what that monster did to you. Get away from her!"

Hades knelt on my other side.

"Touch her and I'll curse all this godsforsaken land to a drought for a thousand years," Mother threatened. She'd do it too. I'd protest if I weren't feeling so weak.

I finally chanced a look down. Blood ran between my fingers where I clutched at my arm. The sight made me woozy. It was one thing to see battered human soldiers, but another to be wounded myself.

"I'll do exactly what I like," Hades quietly told her. He laid a hand over mine, bloodying himself in the process.

Mother stared wet, wrathful hatred at him, but Hades was the most powerful god of the Eight Realms. The threat of a drought wouldn't stop him.

I met his gaze. His intense gray eyes shone glossy. A jolt of fear ran through me. Was I hurt even worse than I thought?

"You have life in your hands," he said gently, removing his own.

My power. I'd forgotten. I could heal myself.

"This is no different," Hades urged.

It felt pretty different to me. Blood loss made me dizzy. Even though, since I was a goddess, I couldn't die, I could suffer as much as anyone else. And this hurt in a squeamish way I didn't want to touch. I felt sick.

"Fix. It." Hades' expression closed, cold and blank. Maybe I'd imagined the shining tears. This was the Hades I'd met in the garden. I wanted to see vulnerable Hades, the one that confessed that he wasn't all-powerful while he pressed his hot lips to my cheek.

Surrounded by the two people I cared for most in the world, I felt alone.

Only I could heal my wounds. They couldn't help. They could just kneel with me, watching.

I sat back and turned to Mother, whose hand found on my skirt-covered knee. If Hades weren't right there, she would have spirited me away to Kantharos that instant. A trip like that would squeeze more blood out of me, but she was desperate enough to do it. I wasn't fit to travel through the air that enormous distance until I did something.

Until I called up the life inside and pulled it to the surface.

I reached down through the ground as I had with the corpses. *No, no, no, not this next part.* Grimacing, eyes shut tight, I trailed a finger through the wound on my arm. With my other hand, I explored the slash in my stomach. Wherever I touched, the muscle and skin knit together. The process was slimy and painful. I fought not to vomit. But it was working.

"That's it," Hades soothed. Suddenly, I wasn't alone anymore.

When I'd finished running my finger along the length of both cuts, I sighed. Opened my eyes. And saw only Mother kneeling beside me, her face frozen in shock.

I twisted to see where Hades had gone. He stood behind me in the big marble hallway, his expression... final.

Mother took my hand in hers, forcing my attention back to her as she checked for injury. Blood coated my fingers, but the wounds were healed. "I'm all right," I said softly.

I'd changed so much that I'd half-expected her to simply *know* when she saw me. It wasn't only my relationship with Hades. She didn't understand I wasn't the same person now that I had been in the royal gardens. That box didn't fit me anymore. And much of that credit went to Hades, because he saw my real power.

"Good," he said. He felt so far away. "I'll lift the wards so you can travel anywhere in the Far Realm directly. I'll still want your help, since your power is the best tool we've found for the human spirits."

His jaw cocked. Obviously, all this extra explanation was for Mother's benefit, although he didn't look at her. Instead, he stared at me.

Something like grief rose again in the depths of his gray eyes.

My throat closed. He wasn't too broken for me. He wasn't too evil. The shadow hadn't meant to hurt me—I knew that as certainly as I knew my own name. Right now, Hades was setting me free so I didn't have to experience pain. Wasn't that kindness?

He placed his hands carefully behind his back. It was a casual pose, one that showed off his power and physique without being obvious, but I saw through it. "It seems clear to me that you're capable of making up your own mind. Come and go as you please."

I opened my mouth but, before I could speak, he was gone.

31

HADES

I knew it.

I fucking knew it.

I'd warned myself every day since I met her, but for some godsforsaken reason I hadn't listened.

I hurt Persephone.

I slammed the door to my office behind me. A second away from destroying my model of the Far Realm, I pulled myself back. That had taken years to construct and was still a work in progress.

My instincts warred.

Destroy.

Save.

I scoffed at myself. Had I really thought that allowing *it*—that dark *thing* was an it now, not a him—to get close to Persephone would end well? If she liked rough sex, I could give that to her alone. I didn't need to split myself in two to satisfy her.

It was just... she accepted the monster inside me. After a while, she wasn't afraid. Earlier, she asked where it was, almost as if she missed it. Someone as bright and beautiful and kind as Persephone liked all of me.

I didn't think that was possible.

And I'd been right. It wasn't possible. Because just now, my dark side had ripped out of my body and injured her in a possessive frenzy.

I did that.

Me.

I hated that shithole side of myself. But I was still a sick fuck, and I already missed both of them—Persephone and *it*. My other self would be banished for a few years, as long as I could stand it, and then something would happen and we'd meld again. I saw the outcome clear as day.

Now that I'd experienced the pain of love, I wanted to drink and drink and drink more of it for eternity. She was branded on my soul, whether or not we could be together.

Stupid—all these poetic thoughts when I had no fucking use for them.

Persephone deserved to be with someone safe, but I'd never forget her.

This was it. No more dreams of some idiotic fairy tale where the three of us co-existed: god of the dead, goddess of spring, and the shadow of my basest impulses.

I hoped she'd come back sometimes. I wasn't kidding about needing her help here. Delicate ecosystem and all that bullshit.

I inhaled slowly, closed my eyes, and exhaled. I had to get a grip.

The Far Realm *was* important to me. Its population of feared, persecuted, and vulnerable beings deserved my attention. This kingdom was my eternal life's work. I'd lost sight of that in the brief time Persephone had upended my world by reminding me in her own way that joy was possible.

At least, I thought so. If I wasn't a cynic before, I was now.

I took four more deep breaths. I'd force myself through the motions of leadership.

When I blew out the last exhale, my eyes were wetter than they should have been. I stalked toward my desk before any of that wetness could crawl down my face. Scowling ferociously, I snatched up the stack of papers on the corner.

Incantation to reinforce walls of Abaddon. Perfect. The prison always had to be maintained. Since I didn't have enough Qa-a-ka memorized, I took the scrap of paper with me as I walked through the air.

My chest heaved as I arrived before the dark, looming walls of the prison. The door was worse off than the last time I'd seen it. My frown deepened. Something had tried to bash it down. The metal bent outward in places and black cracks spread out from it like monstrous spider's legs.

The hulking guards I placed at the entrance swept into quick bows. Their bulk prevented them from doing much more than craning down their necks.

Familiar stress knotted up my shoulders. But at least this was stress unconnected from Persephone and how I could never have her.

This was typical, there's-too-much-and-you'll-inevitably-fail-if-you-pause-to-breathe stress. I straightened my suit, crumpled paper in hand.

Gods, I hated this place. I hated it even more *alone*. The thing inside me provided protection, but it was gone now. Inside there were Typhon (Drakaina's giant mate who nearly

destroyed the gods), Lamashtu (mother of monsters), Hydra...
And those were just a couple of the big ones. Immortal swarms
of venomous spiders, two cyclopes who had been caught after
torturing over four hundred victims for their pleasure—the list
went on. New atrocities. New dangers to the prison itself.

Every minute, these creatures wanted out to rape, torture,
or destroy. They were crafty and powerful. I'd concocted
tortures for the worst of them just so they wouldn't come up
with a way to escape. Eagles tearing at their organs, that sort of
thing. Apart from that early breach, if you didn't count close
calls, my security had held.

"How long since those cracks?" I asked, nodding at the
compromised door. I'd hate to have to replace it.

"A month, Lord Hades," a guard replied.

I grunted. Good thing Persephone wasn't staying. Despite
the beautiful parts of the Far Realm, it was too dangerous.

Which I'd always known.

I paused. Then realized I was waiting for a reply, a voice to
say, *And still we fell in love, didn't we? We took that sweet body she
gave us. We should go get her back. Don't let her get away!*

I smoothed out the incantation and held it up, forming the
first words on my tongue. For a few seconds, it was all gibber-
ish. Persephone was the haze over my eyes. My thoughts were
consumed when I even leaned that way in my mind. I blinked,
and slowly the words came back into focus.

Evil seeped from the prison's pores, growing stronger the
longer I stood there. The deathless inside could tell I was here.
Time to get on with it.

Slowly, and as clearly as I could, I spoke and clicked the
Qu-a-ka words of protection.

The answering *boom* turned even my guts watery. The huge guards flinched as the heavy metallic door crunched and bowed outward.

I set my jaw and finished the last half of the incantation. The monster criminals never liked when I added more security, tethering them to their prison. I'd do it anyway. I'd keep doing it until they were all buried, eternally punished for their unthinkable evil.

Boom!

Boom boom boom boom boom boom boom boom boom...

Screams keened from inside. Snarls. Roars that constricted my throat.

Where was *it*? Something was wrong and I needed my gods-damn darkness.

The incantation. It must have been. I hadn't tested it out first. Had that troll known this would happen if I tried the spell? I would tear him into bloody pieces.

The ground rumbled. The guards brandished their weapons, bracing their feet. It wouldn't matter.

What else could work? What could work? My heart rampaged through my chest. Flipping through my mind for answers was like trying to find a piece of paper in a ransacked warehouse.

I'd used a hundred security measures before on this prison. I wasn't helpless without the shadow. But right now, I couldn't think of a single one.

I squeezed the slip of paper in my fist a second before the next frenzied *boom* erupted around me in a deafening explosion of metal and soil and fire.

32

PERSEPHONE

Mother's warm arms embraced me. I looked over her shoulder at the blank marble wall that marked the end of the fortress corridor.

Why was I so numb?

Mother's hand found the tender place where I'd just healed the wound Hades' shadow had given me.

"Why didn't you tell me?" she whispered.

Which part? "I didn't know until I came here."

She held me at arm's length. Pain and awe warred in her expression. It was hard to look at. "Did you know you could... heal yourself? Not just the flowers?"

"No." I shook my head. Tears welled on my lids. My voice caught when I added, "Hades knew I could."

Mother's beautiful brows knitted together. "Is this his magic somehow?"

"No, Mother." Irritation swirled in with the rest of my roiling emotions. "It's mine. He can't heal himself like this, or reunite the souls. I can. My power is strong enough."

She searched my face as if she wanted an answer to the mystery. But I'd given it to her. I didn't blame her for being confused, though. The last time she'd seen me, I was a different person. I'd dreaded going with Hades, and now...

His shadow had hurt me. I saw his heart shut tight after that. To save me from pain, he hurt me by retreating. I didn't want to be away from him, even with the danger. But he was stubborn, and that look had held all the ancient resolve a god could muster.

A hollow carved into my chest. If I didn't belong at home with Mother, and Hades wouldn't get close to me again, what was I supposed to do?

"My girl," Mother crooned, returning to what she understood, "I missed you."

"I missed you too. And I love you."

"Then let's go home."

I hesitated.

"Lord Hades is gone," she pressed. "Now is the perfect time."

My face felt tight. She didn't understand. Hades wouldn't reappear to claim me, even though I wished he would.

I drew in a deep breath. The gardens weren't bad. I cared for Libera and the rest, even if I was never their favorite. Too wild, they had hinted to me.

They had no idea.

Neither had I, until a few days ago.

I could return to the gardens and my reading shack, spend time with Mother, and then return to help Hades relocate the human souls. I could grow riotous meadows and flowers and woods for them using the energy I reined back in Kantharos.

A rustle sounded down the hallway, like clothes flapping in a breeze.

Marzanna ran toward us. Ran. I'd never seen her look anything but hauntingly dignified. Now she was a ghost fleeing torment.

My blood froze. Mother stiffened beside me with a gasp.

"Marzanna!" I cried. "What—?"

"Get out of here! Go down to the dungeons!" Her shout was unearthly too, like a screaming premonition of death.

"The dungeons?" I managed.

"Now! Hide! Abaddon has been breached!"

Mother convulsively grabbed my arm. "Let's go."

I wrenched away from her, chest heaving, sparkling with dread. "No. You go. Marzanna will show you, or just, go back to Kantharos."

"I won't go without you." Her eyes burned with so much love I was afraid. It was a sticky love. She had to let me go. She had to let me help.

I turned back to Marzanna, who was about to rush past us to warn others. "Is Hades there?"

"I don't know for certain, but I think so."

"I'm going," I told Mother.

"You are not!" she snapped.

"I can help!"

"Abaddon is—"

"I know what Abaddon is! I know *where* it is. And I know I can help." I took one shaky breath. "Please go home. Stay safe."

I walked through the air before she could protest again. This crisis was bigger than disappointing Mother, no matter how much it hurt. My limbs felt bent out of shape. First,

Mother here, then Hades gone, and now the god-prison breached, which meant possible destruction not only for the Far Realm, but the world.

I hoped I was right, that I could do something.

If I were in front of Abaddon and Hades had heard about a breach, he wouldn't stop for a second before running after me.

You have life in your fingers.

I gritted my teeth and landed in front of the prison. Over Hades' unmoving body. He'd been blasted in the chest and head, it looked like. He sprawled with his booted feet facing the wall that now had a smoking hole instead of a door. Long fingers curled around the opening and a spindly being peered out. It didn't look ugly or evil, just strange. But waves of malevolent energy washed out from it.

No no no!

Trembling, I crouched. Life still stirred beneath our feet, even though the air was getting choked with poison. Gods shot out from the prison faster than diving falcons. My heart wouldn't slow. This wouldn't be enough.

I looked at Hades' slack face. It flashed bloody in front of my eyes, changing, morphing, into a hundred different evidences of torture. Psychic manipulation from one of the prisoners. It had to be.

My heart clenched, and I shook my head to clear it. Hades had worked so hard to prevent a breach from happening. His beautiful, terrible Far Realm would suffer if something dramatic didn't happen *now*.

I needed the shadow.

33

DARK HADES

I smell blood.

My blood.

No one harms us and lives! I will rip them to ribbons. I will feast on their bones. But...

He said go. Never come back.

Even now?

I want blood. I taste it. I smell it. I will protect him!

But I feel no thought from him. No call. His order stands.

I hate his order, hate being away from him! I'll look around.

There! There's the blood. There's smoke from an explosion. All monsters set loose!

I am worst of them all. Darkness. God of death. I will make them dead. These claws will tear them out of their immortal bodies because they have hurt us. These teeth will suck their blood.

Call to me. Call to me.

Nothing.

No thought.

I'm stuck. Is he all right? I can't approach until he calls. I'll go mad. I'll tear myself apart. I'll—

A call. I heard it. She said, "Shadow! Come here!"

The girl—Persephone—is part of me too. We're mixed up. The call is strong enough for me to answer.

I dart to her. She stands over our body. My master Hades sprawls on the ground, eyes closed, outside the god-prison. Prisoners stream out. I want to fight, but Hades has no thoughts.

I'm vibrating with tension, growing twice as tall as I fight with my own form. When will he wake up? What can I do?

Persephone moves, not away but closer.

Hades' order holds me back. Stupid order! Persephone's eyes are red and determined. Her body is supple and delicious.

"Shadow," she says.

I loosen, like when Hades gives me more freedom, or I take it. I strain against his order.

It gives.

I bend down, nearly in half, shadows curling like a cloud of smoke, like the smoke rising now from the ruin of the prison. I want to fight. I want to fight.

I want Persephone.

I want. I want. I want.

She reaches out and touches my cheek, her whole palm against my face. My pointed teeth are close to her wrist but she doesn't move away. She looks at my eyes.

This hurts. Different from a fight, it hurts.

I snarl away, but she captures me again. A little goddess, so powerful. It's like she's inside me, moving in my skin.

"I forgive you," she says. "I need you."

Now I want to get inside her. Not my cock (that too) but all the way inside, like I fit in Master Hades' body. In our *body. I belong to her like I belong to us.*

Us is three.

"Help me stop this," she commands.

Yes! I thirst for blood, revenge, and god-fear. I'm ready to destroy everything to obey her.

Her touch against my cheek burns as I grin, mouth open, and rip into the center mass of escaping gods.

❋ 34 ❋

PERSEPHONE

Hades' dark self, three times his normal size and terrifyingly fast, tore through the gods crowding the entrance to the hole. Gods couldn't die, but they could be injured. When the shadow ripped into them, it was carnage.

Evil energy made it hard to breathe. On the ground, Hades didn't stir.

An earth-shaking creak sounded, as if the enormous prison were expanding. Was that the shadow inside? I shuddered. Somehow, I knew it wasn't.

When I touched the shadow, I felt a connection. I knew he felt it too. The ghost of his blood-lust coated my tongue.

And fear. Dread.

Panic.

If Hades' other self was nervous, what was I doing here? Hades was an ancient power greater than Thenios and Ares. And I was a girl who made flowers grow.

I didn't belong here. I'd be torn to pieces.

"Seph! Seph, darling!"

Mother's voice.

I spun. Just behind me stood Mother, ashen. She'd followed me.

No!

I held out my hand to make her stay as another mighty creak wrenched from within the prison. The top of the rust-colored dome was bending outward. Through the hole, I saw something huge moving in the shadows within, stretching the prison itself. Typhon. It had to be. Dread thickened the air around him until the air felt like breathing water.

Typhon, the God-killer.

My eyes darted to Hades, to Mother. Where was Hades' shadow? Still inside, fighting all the criminal gods?

"Shadow!" I screamed. "Get Typhon!"

A roar, deep and bone-rattling as a volcanic blast, exploded from the hole.

"Seph!" came Mother's desperate cry.

"I can't leave!"

I heard my own words. *Then I have to do something.*

I could make plants grow, heal insects and gods, heal souls...

A monstrous hand reached through the gap, taller than me. Slowly, it began to shrink. Typhon was shifting forms. Soon, he would be small enough to fit through.

A black form shot out of the hole, severing one of the tree-trunk-sized fingers. Another roar deafened me as the shadow returned to my side, his fangs dripping with gore.

Mother screamed. But Hades' shadow wasn't our greatest worry. He was our greatest weapon.

"Get the gods who ran," I ordered. I could barely think, I was so afraid. The gods who had escaped so far were enough to devastate the land, and I couldn't catch them.

The shadow sped off in a violent blur.

"We have to close the breach," I whispered to myself, or maybe to Mother. Sucking in a deep breath, I tried to remember Hades' insistence that my power was greater than I believed. That I could do this.

I could do this.

With one last glance at Hades' unconscious face, I turned toward the prison, planted my feet, and screamed. I didn't touch the ground, just reached out my hands like claws. Power pulsed through my veins down to my fingers and the earth responded.

The ground reared up like a tidal wave, trees sprouting along the crest like spines. Tons of soil and roots and green living things piled on the prison. More and more and more. Vines and branches thick with thorns crawled into the hole and over top of the growing mound. A deep, frightening rumble beneath our feet. The smell of fresh-churned earth.

I screamed and screamed and screamed. My sweaty hands trembled but power still rocketed through me. The tall prison rose into the murky sky, somewhere between a hill and a mountain, jutting out from some subterranean, secret place. Life smothered that place of death.

The growth slowed. Pebbles clicked down the mound. Leaves fluttered down after their trees were so violently shoved into the air.

My arms fell to my sides. The ground had moved but now it stopped and that made me dizzy and weak. Or my power did.

But I had closed the prison.

I stood, disoriented, panting, too exhausted to be properly amazed at what I'd done.

Faint sounds of animal struggle in the distance told me Hades' shadow was still hunting down the escaped gods.

Carefully, I turned, feet shuffling, to smile at Mother.

But the sight shocked the smile from my face.

Hades was awake. And he was kneeling.

Pieces of bark clung to the hair of his bent head. His normally pristine, ruthless demeanor melted away. He wasn't clean and he didn't command control.

He was bowing. To me.

"No, Hades..." I began, but I couldn't find the words.

He waved my mother to her knees as well. "Bow to your queen," he said, low and rough and reverent, without looking up.

She didn't look like she needed much prompting. Her skin paled with utter amazement, as if she didn't know me at all.

"Please," I tried again. This was ridiculous. "Get up. I'm just glad you're all right."

Hades raised his eyes—those piercing gray eyes—and pinned me in place with admiration so profound I nearly stumbled back. But he rose, like I asked.

My gut squirmed under all the attention. "Really," I mumbled, "I just had to do something."

"You saved us all," he said. The vulnerability was back in his face, eyes un-shuttered.

"Persephone," Mother breathed. My full name. My real name. She rose too. "I was wrong."

I barely heard the apology, but it was there. "It's not your fault," I said, drawing her into a hug. If I had approached Hades first, I'd never let go.

"It's partially your fault," Hades said, near us.

He added the *partially* for me, because he knew I loved my mother.

She ignored him. "Are you sure you want to stay here?"

I bunched my lips to the side. Obviously, I did.

She understood. Squeezing my hand gently, she kissed my forehead. Fine dirt gritted beneath her lips. I was filthy.

"You are a goddess among goddesses," she whispered. When I was a little girl, she would say that, but now the words felt totally different. Like I was the storybook hero.

I smiled.

And she vanished. Brief worry clung to me. It was a long way back to Kantharos.

My eyes found Hades. "You are not," he said simply.

"Not what?"

"A goddess among goddesses. You are above them."

"Hades..." I didn't want an admirer. I wanted *him*. "I couldn't have done it without... the dark part of you."

Hades' brows ticked downward. "Him? How? I was..." Then a light came into his features. "He listened to you."

I stifled a smile. "He did."

"He belongs to you."

The way he said it gave me pause. "What do you mean?" I asked carefully, although I suspected I knew what he meant.

"He is me."

I swallowed, taking in his beautiful face, hiding such complex layers of darkness and light. "And I am yours."

He didn't move or even change expression. The bravery it

took to say those words felt huge to me, and he gave no reaction?

"I don't care that the shadow hurt me," I continued. "I love you. Both of you."

His gray eyes went vacant for a second, as if he were deciding. Then he stalked forward, falling again on his knees right in front of me. "Then be mine," he said, closing his eyes and pressing his cheek to my stomach. He pressed me close. "I will never want another the way I want you. I will never love anyone more than you. No goddess will live up to you. I want you on a throne beside me. Persephone..." He nuzzled up against me as his words died out.

"I want that," I said, watery and beaming.

He stood and kissed me, a good, firm, possessive kiss that lingered worshipfully at the end. The perfect kiss. As far as innocent kisses went.

"Be my queen."

I grinned up at him. Now that the utter surprise had started to wear off a little, I liked the thought of Hades on his knees.

He seemed to sense my thought, because a smirk twisted his face into something so sexy I felt a little weak. "I promise I'll demonstrate my devotion in whatever way you command."

"Lord Hades," I said. A little jolt told me this was the first time I truly knew I stood on equal ground with him. Hades and Persephone. Too bad I had wasted all that time doubting myself. "I want to express my thanks to your other self for his help today first. Join us."

His smile widened wickedly.

This—he, this place—was more than I'd ever dared to hope

for. A place to belong. The most powerful god in the Eight Realms to love me. And myself, the most powerful goddess.

Future danger didn't frighten me anymore. Together, life would be an adventure.

The rough, beautiful adventure of life and death.

EPILOGUE: PERSEPHONE

"What do you think?" I bounced on the balls of my feet, not bothering to contain my smile.

Hades, dressed in his immaculate dark suit, linked his hands behind his back. The gesture was so familiar that my smile grew. He cocked a brow, observing the plush greenery that gathered in groves and distant patches of wildflowers. I'd even made earthen caves and other interesting features for the spirits to enjoy.

A week after the Abaddon breakout, after Hades' shadow had punished the last of the fugitives and stuffed them back under the mountain I'd created, we found a place for the humans to enjoy an afterlife. Swaths of space. No hostile beings in sight.

"Just because we can't see them doesn't mean they're not there," he had warned me. But after displaying that I could handle myself against the worst gods in history, he let me take this on as a personal project.

I spoke to dozens of humans about what they'd heard about

the afterlife and what they'd enjoy in their eternal rest. For most of them, it was simple—somewhere beautiful with no responsibilities except for spending time with loved ones. I could make that happen.

That was how I found myself tinkering with the finer points of this humungous cave every day for months. The underground cavern itself was so large, it took up half of the Far Realm. I didn't run into any scary creatures (except a basilisk once, but I let it have a separate area.)

Every time I returned to Hades after a long day of work, he seemed relieved to see me. I told him I'd let him see once I was finished. He grumbled that gnomes and other creatures had traveled down there already, and he was King of the Far Realm. I patted him and kissed him and did many other, much filthier things with him whenever I could to soothe his nerves.

The gnomes had come down to offer their expertise in underground lighting—lanterns everywhere, on the walls, in the trees... Everything looked magical. This underworld reminded me of my reading shed in some ways. Wild and homey at once.

Hades rotated, disappeared for a few seconds, returned. "Plenty of space," he said. He'd never paid much attention to these caves because they were made only of barren rock, with no light and little life. A swift, subterranean river lay just inside the entrance too, blocking the way in. The first thing I'd done was commission Tos, the friendly Singer I'd met on my first day, to figure out a way to ferry the spirits across. Before I arrived, this wouldn't have made a good place for the dead humans. But now...

"And?" I prompted.

Hades' look of professional coldness thawed as he met my eye. "And it will do."

"That's it? After all this?" I twirled in my bright pink dress, knowing I matched the pink and white blossoms behind me.

He prowled closer, the epitome of lethal grace. "It's beyond what I hoped for. Centuries will pass before we have to consider any alternative. We can even move my current subjects down here since it's an improvement to where they are now. And the tribes won't have to stay away from the borders. It's astonishing." He hooked a finger under my chin, tipping my head up to look at him. "I think I can't fall more in love with you, and then you do something like this."

My stomach flipped. He could drown me with his gaze and his body, so much larger and more intense than mine. I'd let him.

"The humans will be thrilled to move in tomorrow," Hades said, voice lowered to a seductive growl.

"Tomorrow?" My pulse kicked up between my legs.

He nodded, our heads nearly touching. "You know this place." Suddenly, a dangerous black silhouette appeared over his shoulder. "Think you could run and hide?"

My heartbeat charged ahead before my legs followed. My bare feet drove into the spongey turf. I could have walked through the air, but the challenge was clear.

Run. Hide. Good luck.

With the Realms' greatest weapon on my heels, I sprinted over the hills, avoiding glowing trees, finding dark corners. I sprang behind a riot of hollyhocks as tall as me. The flowers wavered on their stems, but I soothed them with a touch so they'd stop moving.

Heart thumping, I strained to hear. The shadow was silent too. It was too dangerous to look out and see if he was close.

A steel grip on my ankles. I shrieked as my body swept dizzyingly back through the flowers and upside down. I dangled like a fish on a line as blood rushed to my head. My pink shirt didn't cooperate but flounced down over my shoulders.

"She made it too easy!" the shadow complained, shaking me a little.

"Hmm. Yes, she must learn not to do that." Hades strode up slowly, a look of brutal amusement on his face. He took off his jacket and hung it on a nearby tree branch. The muscles in his arms flexed against his sleeves. He tore my dress off the rest of the way and flung it near his jacket.

I was getting dizzy hanging upside down.

"I have an idea." Hades could communicate directly to his shadow without speaking, and I was getting better at sensing what they said to each other. It was like a far-off echo or a memory. Their arousal only made me yearn to know what they'd do to me.

"Yes!" the shadow hissed, dropping me. "I get her first!"

Before I could orient myself, he'd picked me up, the right way up, and sank his fangs into my neck. Just like Dracon and Esmeralda. I hadn't read those books in a while. The real thing was too good.

He groaned against the delicate skin, sucking my blood. His clawed fingers searched me and teased the sensitive nerves between my thighs.

I whimpered, leaning into him.

"Enough noises, darling." Hades removed his clothing in an

orderly way, but as if he was angry he had to be orderly at all. "You'll make me come before I'm inside you."

The claws got rougher, opening up space inside me.

"Please..." I begged.

"What did I say?" Hades' hand was on my jaw. If I disobeyed again, he might grab my hair, which I liked, but I stayed quiet. "On the ground."

The shadow forced me down, never releasing his mouth from my neck, or even the suction. Cool grass dampened my right side.

Hades got down beside us, naked now, skin glistening. "You're going to take both of us today." Without waiting for a response, he grabbed the crook of my leg and pressed it up to my side as he held me open. Both sides of Hades gripped me tight on opposite sides, just like the first time. His cock slid over my entrance, then plunged in.

My gasp obviously excited the shadow, who muttered, "She wants more. Dirty girl."

I was already full of Hades as he found a forceful rhythm, but I nodded. The gesture cut off with a choked cry as he ground against my needy clit.

"Open wide. You're slick for me. Be slick for him."

From behind, the shadow's dick pressed at the skin already stretched around Hades.

"Open," the king ordered again.

They'd both separately practiced stretching me, but now I didn't know if I could do it. My sex felt wet and loose and desperate, but Hades—each of him—was demanding inside me. Both at once...?

Hades slowed. The shadow took his cue, feeding himself in

beside the first hard cock. When he fit more than the head inside, he groaned with satisfaction at the same time I did. The sharp pain subsided little by little. They began to move.

I barely knew what happened next. We were all sweaty. Sometimes one was on top, sometimes another. Brutal, punishing strokes—the kind I liked. Half the time I took both at once, and the other half I split between them. I was pressed into the ground, into a tree, into a firm chest. I ached all over when we finally slowed, then stopped hours later. It was exquisite.

The shadow laughed.

I had bitemarks on my neck.

Hades had a flower in his hair.

THANK YOU!

Thank you for reading *Flowers and the Far Realm*! Please consider leaving a review. Reviews help authors like me get found by more readers.

Now, read on for a sneak peek of a story about Bellona, the war goddess, that will leave you begging for more...

Or, read *Wings and Blindness*—the Eros and Psyche story that ends at the eclipse ceremony that made Hades so uncomfortable at the beginning of this story.

This first book in the Deathless Love series welcomes you to the Eight Realms, where danger and desire lurk in every corner, and mythology isn't quite as you remember it.

Join the Foxy newsletter and read this book FREE!

If anything was going to salvage this godsforsaken trip, it was the male with his fingers around my neck. He didn't know the pulse points and the pads of his hand were soft, but he could squeeze hard enough to cut off air. That left only the pound, pound, pound of him between my legs and the feeling of my back scraping along the tabletop.

The documents under me were useless anyway. I'd spent the better part of today studying the records of Thenios' victory against the Terror. He wouldn't lend them—he was so godsdamn stubborn—and I'd memorized all the battle records at home. I thought that *here,* at the site of the Great Victory, I'd find something, some crumb to give me an edge. Even though Arcan handed me parchment after parchment, book after book, none offered a new approach. After almost a full day wasted, I screamed and threw the nearest offending book against the shelves. The Archives were supposed to house knowledge, not vague praise for the victors without explaining how they'd done it.

I adjusted my chin so I could speak. "You weakling," I taunted.

Arcan hardened his grasp. His silver eyes in a bronze face made for a pretty view as he moved over me. The hand choking me was attached to robe-covered shoulders broad enough to bear arms if he gave up the Archives. Not that I would ask him.

I had my own war to fight, and besides, we'd only seen each other a couple times in our long lives. In general, I demanded texts and he provided them. Today, however, I wanted more and I could see beneath a veneer of apprehension that he wondered what it would be like to have me too.

So here we were. I did unbuckle several knives at my waist so he could pull down my clothes, but I hadn't even had time to take off my metal fingertips before I let him throw me on this table, yank down my leather pants, and plunge inside me.

I liked the slap of him against me but release wasn't close. I had to lose control.

"Slap me," I ordered.

His hand came away with some of the black warpaint I always wore streaked across my face.

"Choke me when—" But apparently he understood because he properly choked me right as his grunts and thrusts grew more frantic.

A book fell to the floor. Hopefully the official account of the Great Victory.

The piercing ache of pleasure finally started to build inside me. I wheezed against his hand.

Bold now, Arcan brought his face close to mine. I bared my teeth and bit at him, missing wide. But at that, he groaned and pulled out just as my own release was cresting. He came into his robe, probably to spare the books or my outfit, still mostly intact.

I sat up, clipping my knives and other weapons back on, disgusted. The intricate braids woven into the hair I wore long between the shaved sides of my head hadn't even come undone.

Arcan adjusted himself, panting, clearly enjoying more satisfaction than I'd gotten. My wire-sprung anger after a fruitless day here only increased.

I gripped the Archivist by the chin with the sharp metal

points of my fingers. "Never leave the Queen of War unsatisfied," I snarled, dragging my dangerous nails across his skin.

His silver eyes went wide, uncomprehending.

He wasn't worth my time. I had bigger worries, like the war over my realm and the audience Thenios demanded with me this evening. If the High King wanted me to help him with another skirmish, so help me, I might blind one of his eyes. No matter that he was my father and the Eight Realms' sovereign. I couldn't bear more of his petty squabbling.

I glanced at the fallen records around the disheveled table, then at Arcan, then marched out to make my meeting with the King.

THIS PLACE WAS SO FAMILIAR. THE SCENT OF HONEY AND mountain air. Gold everywhere. From the tapestries to the stone pillars to the lofted ceilings—everything with my father's symbol of a stylized lightning bolt, of course—each sight brought be back to previous times I'd trod this ground. A thousand memories sliced through my mind: Ares and I playfighting under massive tables, racing to the tallest overlook, competing in holiday challenges...

Why did so many of my memories have to have *him*? I had other siblings. Lox and Vesta. But they were the good children, the obedient, helpful ones. Ares and I made our own chaos. For a time, we were partners.

The images turned sour then ashy in my mouth. I swallowed thickly and raised my chin. That comradery would never be again. I cursed myself for regretting him even for an instant. Traitor.

"Bellona?" I knew the voice like I know my own, the only one I was glad to hear in these halls.

"Mother."

She approached through the abandoned stone hallway with a look of suspicion firmly in place. Mother had three expressions—suspicion, anger, and pride.

The first time I'd beaten Ares in an official training ring, I saw the elusive pride. Mother had bet on me against the King, so I gave her a reason to gloat, to further her own cause in a marriage she hated. Even though I knew the reason for that slight smile, I'd chased that sensation ever since.

Or I did until my life because too full of survival to care about anything else. That was generations of humanity ago.

Mother touched my shoulder, her version of an embrace. She was tremendously tall, taller even than I was, with tan skin and blonde hair. I looked nothing like her. When I was young, I'd even asked if I was one of my father's bastard children, but she insisted Ares and I belonged to her.

"I didn't know you were coming." Her words were laced with underlying theories.

"The High King demanded an audience," I replied, barely keeping my scorn at bay.

Her lips moved as though she were sucking the inside of them. "Has he given a reason?"

"He wants my help for something." It was an assumption, but a good one. The High King envied my armies and war skill.

He also envied everyone else. In his eyes, I ended up as nothing but a tool.

Mother's eyes grew steely with agreement and she nodded. "You're not staying long, I take it."

"I don't plan to." We both knew I couldn't refuse any command outright without risking eternal banishment and imprisonment, but I'd done my share of maneuvering. If I couldn't refuse, I would negotiate terms until the final result equaled refusal anyway. Negotiation wasn't always my strong suit, but we'd done this dance before. I had a lifetime of experience dealing with my father.

"I'm on my way to talk to him now," I said.

Mother drew in a slow breath. "I'll send a cup of spirits to your room in a few hours."

I reached for her hand in thanks, careful not to pierce her with my metal points. She knew I didn't need much—space, competence, and a stiff drink on days like this.

And I needed to get back to my people. They scratched at the edges of my mind, but I couldn't think about them too insistently or rage and fear would choke me more surely than Arcan had. Would they be safe while I was gone?

"I heard about the raid at Ephodia," she said gently, like the feathers on an arrow. She set her jaw. On her, the expression looked regal. On me, it looked threatening. That didn't bother me now, but one day I would reign unopposed. Would I have any sense of royal justice left or only a thick coating of furious bitterness?

"Four hundred sixteen human casualties," I recited. "Three demigods. We got the landing back from him the next day."

"Good." Her elegant brows arched mostly with anger, but I detected a hint of pride.

It wasn't enough to erase the image of the scene I'd encountered two weeks ago. Bloody, mutilated bodies of humans strewn like discarded fish in a market. My healers had only found two clinging to life. They'd both died later. No one to put coins on their eyes and send them to the Far Realm.

The Twin Armies fought again with the bodies still there. The air stank. Birds and scavenging dogs picked at the dead flesh. Yes, I'd regained the landing, but the drive to destroy my brother became a fire that couldn't be pacified by one victory.

When I stumbled upon a pair of twin children, I gave the healers four coins and told them to send the corpses off. Maybe in the Far Realm they could experience a second life to make up for the miserable one they'd lived in my realm of Eriset.

That raid was just one example of why I could not spare another second for my selfish father. An ache pressed against my ribcage, always there but sometimes subdued enough not to feel painful.

"I'm leaving as soon as I can," I said, "but thank you for that drink."

Mother brought her face closer to mine. No one in Eriset dared to do that. "Give him hell," she said, quiet and distinct.

Whether she meant Ares or Thenios the High King, it didn't matter. I was Bellona, goddess of war, queen of bloodshed, conqueror of cities.

Of course I would give them hell.

READ *FLAME AND WARPAINT* NOW!

READ MORE BY ZORA FOX

Fae and Shadow duology
    End of the Forest
    Trapped by the Fae

Deathless Love series
    Wings and Blindness
    Flowers and the Far Realm
    Storm and Sanctuary
    Flame and Warpaint
    Full Moons and Vampires
    Temptation and Tridents
    Candle Wax and Sunlight

Find all of Zora Fox's spicy fantasy romance titles on Amazon.